HER ENDLESS NIGHT

LIARS AND VAMPIRES, BOOK 8

ROBERT J. CRANE

LAUREN HARPER

Her Endless Night

Liars and Vampires, Book 8

Robert J. Crane

copyright © 2018 Ostiagard Press

1st Edition.

1

How long had I been standing here? The darkness surrounded me like a blanket, pressing in from all sides. I could almost feel it as it shrouded my face, obscuring my vision, covering my ears, making me deaf. It was suffocating.

There were no stars overhead, not even one. My heart was in my throat, but my heartbeat in my ears. The tingle of warm, sweaty air lay upon my skin like fresh perspiration, and made me feel like I'd just been for a five-mile run, though I'd been standing here, utterly still, for some time.

The sandy dirt at my feet was still moving.

The lamp on the road that wended its way through the cemetery flickered feebly once, twice, then went out again, leaving me in the darkness.

It was humid. The wind dragged it in off the Gulf of Mexico, making me think of a time in my life that I would never be able to return to; a time where things were fun and carefree. Days when I'd play like a child, chatter like a schoolgirl, and collapse like a teenager only to do it all over again tomorrow.

But now...it felt like there were no more tomorrows.

I was standing over the grave of my best friend...

...Who was now clawing her way out of the dirt.

At least...that's who I assumed it was. I hadn't had the pleasure of meeting a vampire before they were turned as well as after. I had no idea how any of this worked. Who was it that was going to be coming out of the grave?

I'd never thought that I'd have to watch a friend of mine be laid to rest. Death was a far-off thing, for old people, like my parents and grandparents. Not for kids like me, still in high school, still young, still with life in front of them...

But there had been no more life in front of my best friend Xandra. Hers had ended at the hands of my former best friend, Jackie. I'd cried when we found her. Begged for it not to be the case. Wished she could still have just one more day, one perfect, golden day where we went to the beach, shopped at the mall, laughed over stupid TikToks in a perfect silly world of our own making.

A world where vampires didn't exist.

Now I couldn't help but think...it would have been so much better for her if she just stayed dead.

The shifting earth smelled strongly of mud and rotten leaves. Pale purple hair, mussed with clumps of dirt, appeared between the grains, closely followed by pale, filthy fingers.

My stomach reached the peak of the roller coaster track it was on...and dropped.

I never thought I'd see her again. Hope collided with terror, tumbling in my chest, vying for control.

Should I run?

No. I needed to stay with her.

Should I embrace her?

No. It was likely I'd have to defend myself against her.

Was she going to be thirsty when she woke up? Will she even know what she was supposed to do in this new...form?

I had seen the beast in Mill. Is this who Xandra was going to be? Nothing more than a blood-sucking monster?

Or would she be Iona, one who could control her nature, who hated the very fact of what she was?

A nagging voice at the back of my head reminded me that neither of them had ever really told me what it was like when they turned. It was almost like it was a taboo subject, a time in their existence that they would rather not remember.

My grip tightened around the cool wood of the silver-tipped stake in my hand.

If push came to shove...could I actually kill her?

Who was I kidding?

I already had.

More of her hair appeared, and my heart gave an uncomfortable lurch.

Sunshine and laughter filled my mind. Xandra and I, sitting on the porch of that little restaurant on the beach, sipping fruity, slushy drinks, watching people walk by.

"Come on, you have to go to FSU with me," Xandra was saying. "Who else am I going to room with? No one is going to put up with my anime addiction."

"But that's still a year away," I said. A lifetime, really.

"You haven't thought about this at all, have you?"

I had shrugged. "I have...but I just don't know what to do." I'd always thought I'd go to a SUNY school. But that was before the lying came out, before my life was ruined, before my parents retreated to Florida to give me a fresh start and hide my shame.

"Come with me," she said with a big grin and a toss of

her periwinkle hair. "And we will figure it out together. As Seminoles."

My eyes stung as I stood at her graveside, staring down at the fingers groping their way through the dirt. I could hear the earth shifting as she dragged herself out.

The light along the road flickered into life again, helping me to see her better, making the shadows darker, the paleness in her skin even more evident.

Was she going to be a beast, like Mill? Or a steady, even presence that rose, steel keeping back the horrors within so I barely ever saw them?

I swallowed nervously. What if it was Xandra unleashed that appeared? What if she was Jacquelyn part two, hating the very sight of me, blaming her turning entirely on me, on fire with the sole purpose of getting revenge on me for all of the suffering I had put her through?

I shifted my footing, rolling the stake in my sweating palm.

Now I could see her forehead, her brow line rising out of the earth, and then the rest of her face appeared like a flower bursting from the frozen ground during spring's first thaw. She shook her head, sending dirt flying. I didn't move. I was frozen to the spot.

She opened her eyes, blinked them a few times, squinting as if she were staring up into the brightest sun...

And our eyes met.

My stomach sank. They were still the same icy blue, but they were...different somehow. Cold. Lifeless.

Had the bright, excitable, snarky Xandra really died? Was this...thing in front of me nothing more than a husk of what once was?

The sorrow that filled me was even more potent than

what I had been nursing for the last three days. It was almost as if it were real to me for the first time.

My eyes stung as I stared down at her.

The girl who had just appeared from the depths of the grave cocked her head to the side, staring up at me. It sent chills down my spine.

It wasn't Xandra. It may look like her, it may even be lying in her grave. But it wasn't her. It couldn't be. And I gripped my stake tighter, preparing to plunge it into my former best friend's chest, into her now-dead heart.

Of all the nightmares and dreams I'd had since I'd found Xandra dead, nearly all had involved a moment like this. Her come back to me, the consequences of my terrible loss all wiped away. I'd pictured a sun-drenched reunion, bright and happy and endlessly cheery.

This was not the reunion that I had secretly been hoping for.

"Cassie?"

The voice that left her parted lips was scratchy...like she hadn't used it in a thousand years.

2

"Xan...Xandra?" I said. My voice cracked, too. I blinked at her a few times.

She...recognized me.

My deepest fear had been that she would have somehow forgotten her life, lost her memories, never even realized that she had been a human before. I kept telling myself that maybe they would come back eventually, that she wouldn't always be this blank slate in the body of person that I cared so much about but had completely forgotten about me.

"What...what happened?" Xandra asked, bringing one of her hands up to the side of her face, like her head was suddenly throbbing. Fingers disturbed the grains of earth clinging to her pale skin. Her eyes closed and her brow furrowed. "I...I can't really remember anything. Where...am I?"

I swallowed, my throat as dry as the Sahara. "You don't remember?"

"I remember being in the limo...with you, and Mill. Then I remember that big house. We talked to that British guy – what was his name? V something..."

Her voice sure sounded the same, and it made my heart ache.

She pressed both of her hands on the ground on either side of her, pushing herself out of the ground.

My heart clenched as I caught sight of the dress that she had been buried in. It was the one that she had worn the night we went to see the play – the night that Jacquelyn and Varycas's vampires had hunted us through downtown Tampa.

She was halfway out of the earth now. It was like she was standing in a pool made of dirt.

"Something happened," she said, brush stray grains from her face. "I remember screaming, and running, and–"

She looked up at me.

"I remember you."

This was a lot harder than I ever thought it might have been. In all of the scenarios I had played out in my head, it was never, *ever* this painful.

My knees buckled as I looked at her. It was taking all of my mental guarding, months of being submerged in the world of vampires, to keep me from throwing myself at her feet and begging for her forgiveness, telling her all of the things I had wanted to say. To tell her how important she was to me...

...How I didn't know how I was going to live through the rest of my life without my best friend.

Her eyes darted downward for a fraction of a second, and it took me a moment to realize that she was glancing at the stake still clasped tightly in my hand.

"What am I doing...in a cemetery?" she asked, eyes slowly crawling back up to mine.

"You don't remember what happened?" I asked. "What Varycas–"

My tongue was suddenly knotted. I couldn't tell her. I couldn't bring myself to admit it.

But it wasn't like I really had time, because with one last, furtive glance at the stake in my hands, she leapt out of the grave.

I was glad that I hadn't completely let my guard down, but she had lulled me into enough of a sense of security that she was able to wrap her fingers around my throat.

I gasped, trying to pry her hands away, but before I could reach my neck, her other hand darted out with incredible speed and strength, yanking my arm away from me.

Pain shot up my arm as she held it out straight. She squeezed my wrist until my fingers crumpled, and the stake tumbled out of my hands into the grass.

My heart was hammering inside my chest, like a woodpecker against an ancient tree. I was breathing fast and heavy.

Not a sound escaped from Xandra's mouth. Her heart was cold and dead in her chest.

She had disarmed me. I was entirely at her mercy.

"I remember everything," Xandra whispered.

3

Xandra's newfound vampire strength was unbridled. I was used to vampires being fast and strong, but their movements were always controlled, planned. Xandra was still sluggish, jerky in her movements, unaware of how strong she really was.

I pulled at her hand, closing around my throat. It was like trying to pry iron; immovable, steely, slowly clenching. I could barely breathe, the gasps more like wheezes. "Xandra–" Stars were flickering in my vision. "Please – I –"

There was no one around. Iona was gone. I had chased Mill off. Lockwood was outside the cemetery, waiting for me. He wouldn't find me until it was too late.

Stupid. Arrogant. I'd put myself in this situation, and I had no one to blame but me.

No extra stakes. The holy water in the holster on my thigh under my dress was out of reach.

The pain in my arm grew as she pulled it farther from me. She was looking at me like a scientific specimen, a growing hunger in her eyes as she awoke to her true nature.

My feet dangled beneath me, barely scraping the grass that was starting to collect dew.

Nothing that Mill or Iona had taught me would be able to help. I had never fought a freshly changed vampire, one that had gotten the upper hand before I even had a chance to react.

And it was *Xandra.* How in the world could I fight her, even if I knew I had to?

My mind was fogging, like fog pressing in on my thoughts.

"You left me behind, Cassie," Xandra whispered, like wind through the wet grass.

That cleared my head with a shocking clarity, focused me like a punch to the gut.

I looked at her, and I could have sworn I saw something different there. Something that was totally unlike Jacquelyn. Where Jacquelyn was fueled by hatred, all I could see was loneliness in Xandra's eyes.

"Xandra – I – I'm sor–" Choking the words out around her hand on my throat was nigh impossible. Her grip was like iron, and tightening with every moment.

I'd never wanted to leave her. I hated Mill for dragging me from Varycas's house. I would have stayed behind and died, gone to the grave with Xandra. Together in death, that's what we would have been. Rising together, too, maybe. I never wanted this. I never–

Something slammed into Xandra, something flashing in the dark like molten gold.

It was as if I had just broken the surface of the water after a long drowning; I gasped, drawing in what felt like the first real breath of my life.

At the same time, I tumbled to the ground as Xandra

had dropped me. I landed hard, rolled onto my side, massaging my throat, but not wanting to turn my back to Xandra.

Who was it? My heart thumped painfully. Possibilities rolled over me like crashing waves on the Sarasota beach. It must have been Iona. She had come back, knowing it was possible she was going to rise like this. Or maybe Mill. Even though I had ended things, he wouldn't have wanted me to be defenseless, right? Jed could have stuck around. Maybe he decided to keep an eye on me until he was sure everything was safe. Or Lockwood. He was closest, after all. Maybe he was wondering what was taking so long.

I pushed myself up onto my knees and saw a dash of purple as Xandra disappeared into the shadows of the cemetery behind shadowy tombstones and stray, looming trees. She faded into the night, the color of her hair disappearing into the gloom.

And gold remained. "Oh, no..." I groaned.

Standing beside the unearthed grave was a woman in a gold silk dress, tall, thin, with long gilt hair that flowed over her shoulders as if it had a life of its own. Wings sprouted from her back, like a butterfly, shimmering softly in the dimness. When she looked over at me, she smiled, and I saw the black pupils surrounded by the liquid gold irises.

Gratitude vanished, and in its place came a sinking feeling of utter dread.

What the hell was *she* doing here?

"Orianna..." I pushed up from the dewy grass. "You...? What – what are you doing here?"

"I'm glad you asked, and that I could help you just now," she said. Her wings fluttered their last and disappeared as if they'd been sheathed. With the grace only a Fae could muster, she planted her fists on her hips and smirked at me, mischief dripping from it, and the surety of one who knew I now owed her a favor. "Because as it turns out...now I need *your* help."

4

"Help?" I asked, my head still slightly floating, slightly aching from the oxygen deprivation of Xandra's MMA-style chokeout. "You need *my* help?"

"Yes." Orianna stepped closer to me, back into the light of the lamps. Her eyes glowed – hell, damned near all over glowed – the dress, the hair, her very skin. In the land of Faerie, the golden look seemed to fit. Here on Earth, though, she looked like some avant-garde model on her way to a fashion show where the theme was precious metals.

"No," I said. I didn't even think about it. The word just slipped out before I had even considered the full implications of what her appearance on Earth could mean.

Her eyes narrowed. "What do you mean, no? I just helped you. And I haven't even told you what I need yet."

"Just that," I said. My emotional tank was on E, and while her sudden appearance might normally have elicited a different reaction, I barely had the energy to react. "No means no. I am not going to help you. I can't, and I won't."

"I don't understand," Orianna said, shaking her golden

head. "After everything that we went through together, you don't even want to listen to what I have to say?"

"Listen," I dusted off my knees, realizing that Mom was going to kill me for ruining the funeral dress we bought. Correction. Xandra ruined the dress that I wore for *her* funeral. Since it was for her, it seemed somehow sporting to me. Doubt Mom would see it that way, though. "It's great to see you and everything, but my best friend just became a vampire. She literally just came out of the grave right in front of you."

"Best friend?" Orianna asked. Her eyes were narrowed, her mind processing this development. "I've never heard of such a thing..."

"And while I appreciate you making sure she didn't suffocate me, I need to find her." I finished dusting myself off. The dress was ruined. Stain stick would find it had no power here, for dirt had won the day. "By the way, since I'm an ingrate already, did you see which way she ran off?"

"She's gone," Orianna said, gesturing off into the shadows. "This was your friend?"

"She is–" I started, and then huffed. "She was. Is. I don't know." My head was still woozy from being choked. I scanned the darkness covering the cemetery and rubbed my dirty hands on my forehead. "Great. I'm going to have to find a way to deal with her later." And I started toward the gate where Lockwood was waiting.

"Wait, I need your help," Orianna said, trailing behind me.

I stopped and held up my hand to stop her. "Listen, I really can't help you right now. Vampires just started a war in my city, and it's kinda turned everything upside down. Hence the girl coming out of the grave."

"Miss Cassandra," a voice called. Turning, I saw Lockwood hurrying between the gravestones. "Are you all r–" His voice trailed off as his eyes fell on Orianna, who was fluttering just feet above the ground. I didn't have the energy to tell her that she shouldn't be doing that in the human world. "What is *she* doing here?"

"Well, if it isn't the heroic Paladin," said Orianna with a wide, flashing grin. She tilted her head to the side, and pressed the tip of her finger to her lips in concentration. "Where are your wings? And why is your hair different?"

Lockwood ignored her and turned to me. "Are you all right? Why is your dress filthy? Your mother will not be pleased."

"Add that to the list of things my mother will not be pleased about," I said, rubbing my neck. "I'm sure it'll sandwich nicely between all the lying and the kidnapping she endured at the hands of Byron."

"What's wrong with your throat?" Lockwood asked.

"Xandra," I said.

He looked as if he swallowed his tongue. "Miss Alexandra...but she was – "

"Well, she's not anymore," I said, pretty well kicking myself. "She's been turned."

Lockwood took a step back, running his hands through his dark hair. "I am so terribly sorry, Cassandra. That's why you wanted to stay, was it? You were worried that she–"

"I should have seen it coming," I said. "Jacquelyn hates me. Why go for the kill when you can cause so much more pain with one ill turn?"

"The girl attacked as soon as she was out of the soil," Orianna said. "Threw herself right at Cassie, hands around her throat. If I hadn't been here to intervene, then who knows what might have happened." She folded her arms, beaming at us.

Lockwood looked at me.

"Yes, she did save me," I said. "Xandra took me off guard."

"I'm sorry I didn't come sooner," Lockwood said, putting a hand on my shoulder. "I did not wish to intrude upon your grief. I gave no thought to Miss Alexandra turning, and I should have."

"We all should have," I said softly. "Me more than anyone."

"It seems you're having some personal problems," Orianna said, stepping between Lockwood and me, elbowing his arm off my shoulder. "But I really need your help, and it's way bigger than petty issues between night-bloods and iron bearers. Please."

I could see the pain in her eyes, and where I probably would have once cared, I just felt frustration now. Frustration, and exhaustion.

"Winter is in crisis," Orianna said.

I stared at her blankly. "It's summer."

"The Winter *Court,* Cassandra," Lockwood said, sotto voce.

"I know what she meant," I said. "There's a baby fledgling vampire that's rolling through Tampa wearing my former best friend's skin right now. I have neither the time nor the energy to deal with Fae and their ill-weather courts." I started to walk away.

"Summer is diminished," Orianna said, trailing me. "Winter is rising because something has happened."

"What has happened?" Lockwood asked. He was following me, but listening to her.

"We don't know," Orianna said. "There has been no communication between Summer and Winter since the

confrontation that the two of you so bravely turned around."
Was that sarcasm? It almost sounded...sincere.

"How long ago was that?" I asked, not daring to turn, for
fear I'd get sucked into this drama.

"It's been years now," Orianna replied. Time was wonky
on Faerie. "With Summer's diminishment, we've had to take
up the slack. Now the boundaries with Earth are bleeding
thin."

As if on cue, there was a sudden rush of cool air. It
hadn't dropped below ninety in the last three weeks...did
someone nearby roll down their windows with their AC on
full blast?

"Nope, I don't want to hear it," I said, holding up my
hand and walking toward the gates. "I have too much going
on. I can't help."

Lockwood's footsteps followed after me.

"Lockwood, did you see her?" I asked.

He shook his head. "The first I heard of her was when I
walked up here and found you in this state."

I sighed. It was too much to hope that this would be easy,
that one thing in my life could go right in the last week...or
in the last several months, really.

"But...I need your help," she called after me, her voice
soft and pitiful.

"Get someone else to help you," I said, striding away,
decision made. "Come on, Lockwood. We have to find
Xandra."

5

I climbed into the passenger seat of Lockwood's car with a heavy sigh. It was like my heart was encased in an iron cage, heavy and impenetrable. How could I feel so much in one second, then nothing the next? Mom had said numbness was a part of the grieving process. How was I supposed to grieve at the grave of someone who was no longer buried there?

"Let us take a loop around the cemetery," Lockwood suggested. "See if she is hanging around somewhere."

I didn't reply.

We made a full lap around the place, and some of the side streets nearby. It was so dark, it was impossible to see anything. And Xandra wasn't likely to be strolling along the sidewalk without a care in the world. The sidewalks were quiet, the only sound rustling leaves in the suddenly chill breeze. It seemed to be coming out of the north, no touch of the Gulf of Mexico to warm it.

"Are you all right?" Lockwood asked after some time had lapsed and we had settled into an uneasy silence.

I sighed. How was I supposed to answer that question

anymore? "I don't really know. Everything just feels so...so unreal. I can't believe any of this." It even sounded weird to say it out loud. Glad it wasn't just in my head.

"You never voiced your fears about this happening," Lockwood said. "Yet you must have been sure, to stay as long as you did at the grave."

I sighed. "I was worried about it being Jacquelyn all over again...and I was totally right."

"We'll find her," Lockwood said. "We just have to keep looking."

"We aren't going to find her," I said, shaking my head. He looked over at me, concern written all over his face. "She's gone." He made a sound, noncommittal, but clearly holding some deeper meaning. "What?"

He glanced over his shoulder before changing lanes. We were on one of the main roads now, and he navigated traffic with flawless ease. "Orianna appearing," he said. "It is an ill bit of news."

"We keep saying 'ill' tonight," I said. "Ill omens, ill met, I think I'm going to be...everything's ill, and not in the way gangstas mean it." I stared out of the window into the darkness as we passed a Burger King. Worry tightened the knot in my stomach. As much as I didn't want to admit it, Orianna's problem *did* bother me, and I was thinking about it in the back of my mind regardless of whether I wanted to or not. "What do you think about what she was saying?"

Lockwood slowed as we came to a stop sign, looking at the other car across the intersection, waving him through. "It bodes...well, you know the word."

"'Wonderful?'" I asked, with exaggerated enthusiasm. "It bodes 'marvelous,' surely. It heralds great things, like unicorn cupcakes, and the arrival of gallons of pho from Xandra's mom's ramen shop. Pretty balloons for everyone."

Lockwood's smile was laced with irony. "If only."

I looked out of the window, my heart sinking. I kept hoping I'd see a whisper of purple hair, a glimpse of her dress. "Why would Orianna need me, though? When she has the entire Winter Court at her back?"

Lockwood huffed air through his nose as he eased onto the accelerator again. "I have long since stopped questioning your peculiar place in the firmament of the paranormal." Now his smile was mysterious, and almost sweet. "You seem to have a great knack for this, in spite of your wish that you had remained untouched by it all."

"Yes, I've been thoroughly touched at this point," I said, folding my arms across my chest. "Punched, slapped, knocked around – frankly I could go for a pat on the head as a change of pace."

"I think it unlikely you will find that should you choose to give aid to Orianna," Lockwood said. "If she is here, she has need of your talents."

"What talents?" I asked, groaning.

"Your ability to lie was second to none when we were there," Lockwood said.

Another groan. "I put that part of my life behind me. I'm trying to be honest now. Forthright. Almost saintly."

"I am aware," he said.

"This could not have happened at a worse time," I said. "It's like they looked at my calendar, saw 'Trouble' written on every day, and wanted to add more to it."

"You seem to have a knack for attracting that as well, don't you?" he said, his smile fading.

"Yes," I said. "And I'm knackered out on it – all of it. Let's just keep going. Maybe we'll see her."

We kept driving.

We didn't see her.

6

"Let's just go home," I finally said. My heart was heavy, and if I was honest, so were my eyelids. I needed to sit, to think. The car was rolling through the quiet suburban streets, darkness a heavy pall around us. He'd turned off the air conditioner a few miles back, because the temperature in the car was curiously falling.

"Are you sure?" Lockwood asked. He stared at me with a quiet curiosity, his green eyes luminous even in the dark. He was at my command, as ever.

"Yeah," I said. "After one more stop."

"You name it," Lockwood said.

"Maybe she went back to her house," I said. "I doubt it, but it's the only place left I can think of."

"Very well," Lockwood said. We were almost to my neighborhood, stopped at a traffic light. I looked up; a car stopped on the eastern side of the intersection.

I squinted.

"What is it?" Lockwood said.

"Is that...?" I asked. It certainly looked familiar. An older Honda Civic, dark green, was stopped there. "I think that's

Derrick's car." I leaned forward in the seat, trying hard to see into the dark interior of the Honda.

"It certainly looks like his," said Lockwood. "Though that is a common enough model."

We pulled closer. It was his car. There was the dent on the left side of the hood from where Gregory tried to be cool and skidded across the front of it, but instead just bounced across in pain because of how hot the metal was. Florida in the summer. It'll burn your ass. They ought to put that on all the tourist brochures.

"There's someone in the front seat with him," I said. The light turned green on their side of the street, and they turned onto the road that we were on, heading south. Lockwood and I both leaned toward the window, staring through. I could see Derrick driving, and in the passenger seat... "*Jed*?!"

"What?" Lockwood asked.

Sure enough, I saw Jed's Amish hat (I don't know what they're called) in shadow as they passed beneath a street lamp. "What in the world are they doing out at this hour?"

"Perhaps Derrick saw him at the funeral and asked him if he wanted a ride," Lockwood said smoothly. The light finally turned green on our side, and Lockwood continued forward.

I didn't have much time to contemplate this odd turn of events, but it was probably good that Jed and Derrick were becoming friends. We turned down onto the street where Xandra's house was, and I felt my heart bubble up into my throat.

I had purposely avoided this street since I had found her body. After what her parents said at the funeral, I didn't want them to see me anywhere near their house. The thought of talking to them, of somehow involving myself in their misery? It made me sick, threatened to capsize me in a sea of emotion from which there was no rescue.

Lockwood pulled up in front of her house, the headlights off. It was really hard to look at the place. Too many memories. The light in her room was off, the place where we'd shared so many late-night gabfests talking about anything and everything. Her front porch where we sat eating coconut popsicles while they dripped all over our hands in the scorching heat. The car we would drive around in during the blissful weeks of summer vacation sat in the driveway, silent.

My throat was tight.

Why had I taken her for granted? She had been one of the brightest spots in my life, and she had been ripped away from me.

My hand went to my throat, wondering if I'd have a ring of bruises by morning. I never thought she would ever try to strangle me. I wasn't sure if I'd be able to sleep for the next few nights without my dreams being filled with her face, surrounded by darkness, the cold, lifeless eyes staring into mine.

"Do you really think that she would come here?" Lockwood asked, his voice barely a whisper.

I had really hoped she would. I wanted it to be that easy. I finally shook my head. "No, she must realize that coming back to a place like this would make her easier to find. And if she ran off, she doesn't want to be found."

She doesn't want to be found.

Why did that feel like a knife in the gut, followed by a sharp twist?

"I don't know," I said. "I really don't know her anymore, I guess."

Lockwood pushed the accelerator, and the car purred away from the curb. I didn't stop him.

As we were heading back toward my house, I pulled my phone out of my purse that I had left in Lockwood's back seat, opened the messages, and clicked on Iona's name. *Call me ASAP,* I texted, then hit SEND. I sighed, sinking back against the seat.

"I just want you to know," Lockwood said, his dark hair gleaming as he passed a street lamp, "that while I do not know exactly what you are feeling right now, I am here for you. If you need anything, or wish to talk about any of this, please do not hesitate to ask. All right?"

I looked over at him, and felt my lip quiver just a hint. "Thanks, Lockwood."

We pulled up outside my house. The lights were still on inside. I wasn't surprised. Mom and Dad wouldn't have gone to sleep until they knew I was home safe. Force of habit now, I guess.

I opened the door and stepped out into the night, the overwhelming quiet surrounding me. A little brisk air came whipping through as I went, pushing chill bumps out on my skin. He opened his, as if to walk me to the front step, but I said, "No, Lockwood, it's okay. You should go home. Get some rest."

He gave me a questioning look. "Are you sure you do not want me to...hang around? Keep an eye out?"

"It'll be fine," I said. "Whatever happens with Xandra, I'll be ready for her."

"That smacks to my ears of bravado," he said. "You have already had one terrible encounter with Xandra. Varycas and Jacquelyn remain out there. Your safety is of paramount concern to me."

"You've been hanging around for days, Lockwood," I

said, feeling desperately weary. "Aren't you tired? I know I am. I just texted Iona. And you're not that far away. If anything crazy happens, I can call you. Besides, I don't think she's going to come for me now anyway." I looked up and down the street; there was no hint of life save for that chilly wind.

He studied me for a minute, debating about whether or not to ignore my request and come inside with me anyway. "All right," he said at last. "Promise me that you will call. For any trouble, no matter how mild."

"Got it," I said. "Kinks in my hair I can't get out with a brush, I call you. Done."

His eyelid twitched slightly. "I am not certain I would be of much use in that circumstance, but I suppose it better to err on the side of caution."

"If I can't get my bagel evenly sliced," I said, with great seriousness, "I will not hesitate to call you. A Paladin is good with a blade, right?"

"Oh," he said, "you are mocking. I see it now. Nonetheless I will take that as a faerie promise that should you encounter true, genuine difficulty—"

"Sometimes I have trouble getting the lid off the pickle jar," I said, keeping from smirking only by dint of pure exhaustion. "And you're so strong, Lockwood—"

"A fae promise, Cassandra," Lockwood said, so very serious. "You know what it means."

"I break it at my own great peril," I said, sagging against my front door. "You get my firstborn or something. Very Rumpelstiltskin-y."

He straightened immediately. "How do you know Rumpelstiltskin? Have you already made a bargain with him?"

"Go home, Lockwood," I said, fumbling with my keys. I

pushed the door open, waving him off. "I will call you if I have difficulty, and I will make no fae bargains nor engage in any battles nor open any pickle jars without your aid. Good night, and please get some sleep." I closed the door on his worried eyes, watching me.

I knew that I wouldn't call him. I needed him to rest. It couldn't have been easy, having to deal with the bundle of jagged nerves I'd been since Xandra's death. He'd been diligent, ever-watchful, protecting my family and I while we grieved.

Now that everything had changed, *again*, I needed him to be in top form in case things went south...*again*.

From the window I watched him go, then walked back to the door and threw it open, sighing into the chill breeze. "Are you just going to hover up there all night like I can't see you?"

Orianna drifted down in front of me, hovering just above the ground, golden wings fluttering behind her like a butterfly. "I can't leave without your help."

I could see from the pained look on her face that she was completely serious. I mean, she wouldn't have followed me halfway across the city if she didn't really need my help, right? As I stood under the clouded sky, I had to wonder...how did a compulsive liar from New York get so wound up in the lives of all these mythical creatures?

Before I could answer, the phone in my hand buzzed, making us both jump. Orianna flittered up five feet, her eyes growing round as she looked down at it. "What is that mystical light?"

"It's called a cell phone," I said. Iona was calling. "Stay away from it. I hear you break them," I answered and pressed it to my ear. "Hey, Iona."

"Who are you talking to?" Orianna asked, still keeping her distance. She looked like a cat, ready to hiss at it.

"What have you gotten yourself into this time?" Iona asked. No preamble, just that.

"I have done nothing," I said. "I swear."

"I know you haven't done anything," Orianna said. "You haven't agreed to help me. And why won't you look at me when you are talking to me? It is very rude."

I glared at her, and her brow furrowed.

"Then why in the world did you need me to call you?" Iona asked.

"I need you over here right now," I said.

"Why?" Iona asked.

"I'm already here," Orianna said. "Why do you have that *sell fun* pressed to your face? Is it magical? Does it warm you in this chill eve?"

"Something happened, and I need your help," I told Iona, holding my hand up in Orianna's face as she drifted in to look at my phone more closely.

Iona didn't even hesitate. "I'm on my way." And she hung up. I slid my phone back into my purse.

"I'm very confused," Orianna said, coming back to the ground, her wings losing their gleam and fading away as she landed. "What just happened?"

"You really are lost in this world, aren't you?" I looked at her. If she followed me all across Tampa, it was likely she wasn't going to just leave now. The wheels in my mind were spinning slowly, but looking into her strangely slit pupils, I felt my resolve fade.

I didn't have the heart to kick her out right now. There had been too much suffering going on around me lately. Besides, Iona was on the way. If I needed to eject Orianna out onto her ultra-thin fae derriere, I had no doubt she would do it with plenty enough gusto to see the unseelie gone for good.

"All right, you," I said, my words dragging as the fatigue settled on me like lead on my bones. "No point in just hovering out here." I stood aside, beckoning her forward. "Come in."

7

"Hey guys, I'm home," I called out as Orianna stepped into the house behind me. I shut the door so she wouldn't have to touch the knob. Not being a metallurgist, I had no idea if it was iron, and I decided better safe than listening to her scream as her hand burst into flames. It was surprisingly warm inside, which was an immediate comfort. The house smelled of lavender and vanilla with a hint of smoke; Mom must have just blown out her favorite candle.

Orianna's nose twitched as I led her through to the kitchen. She looked ready to say something, but she kept her powder dry on the way through, her wings now invisible, and looking (almost) human.

I pushed through the door into the kitchen, which was pristinely clean, as usual. Dad's favorite tea mug sat next to the sink, the bag still dangling over the edge, string hanging onto the counter. As I scanned the room, my heart jolted when my eyes caught on the order of service for the funeral sitting on the island beside Mom's purse. Xandra's smiling face stared up at the ceiling from the front page.

I'd taken that picture of her only a few weeks ago. The

lump in my throat made it hard to breathe. Mom and Dad were sitting at the table in the dining area, and had looked up when we stepped inside. They didn't say anything, but their gazes had both settled on the stranger in the room. "This is Orianna," I said. "She's from Faerie."

Mom blinked at me, and Dad tilted his head slightly to the side. "...I beg your pardon?" Mom asked.

Orianna's wings appeared behind her, fluttering nervously. "Who are these people? Are they your servants?"

"These are my parents," I said.

"Oh, I have those as well," Orianna said. She beamed at my parents. "How very nice to meet you."

Mom's eyes were on Orianna's wings. "She's a faerie? Like Lockwood?"

"Yeah," I said, giving a look at the golden, wings-fluttering fae beside me, "but Orianna's not wearing a glamour."

Dad had taken his glasses off and was rubbing his eyes. Mom had folded her arms across her chest, arching a brow. Uh, oh. Lawyer mode. "So we left you at the cemetery...and you bring home a faerie?" Mom asked. "I mean...why?"

"She just showed up," I said, then halted. Maybe it wasn't the best idea to tell them about Xandra...yet. One new mythical creature at a time. Also, Mom was going to freak, and I just didn't want to deal with that.

"And you brought her here?" Dad asked.

"Well, yeah," I said. "I didn't really have a choice. She kind of followed Lockwood and I here."

"Where is Lockwood?" Mom asked, she was looking around like she expected him to jump out of the breadbox. Which may have been technically possible, with fae magic, but hopefully he was home, sleeping rather than hanging out with our moldy wheat bread and day-old bagels.

"I sent him home," I said.

Her face fell somewhat. Dad's, too. That was odd. Did they actually want Lockwood to stick around? I mean, I knew it was nice to have the protection, but had they come to depend on it already?

"What's going on?" I asked, with an all too familiar sinking feeling. "You two look pretty grim, even for having attended a funeral today."

They glanced at one another, and then both looked in Orianna's direction. Clearly no one wanted to say anything with a stranger in our midst. I sighed. "All right, give me a second. Come on, Orianna, I'll show you my room."

"*Your* room?" Orianna asked, wings fluttering. "How exciting." I led her past Mom and Dad, her eyes combing over every surface, every object, soaking it all up like a dry sponge in a puddle.

We made our way up the stairs. I pushed open the door to my room, and Orianna was positively quivering with anticipation. She darted inside past me, landing in the very center, staring around as if she were in the most interesting place she had ever been.

"What is this?" she asked. She snatched up the stuffed bear that Laura had won at the state fair we had gone to together. "It resembles a creature. But it's not moving."

"It's stuffed."

"Stuffed?"

"Not real," I said.

She nodded and set it back on the bed. Her eyes widened as they fell on the collection of perfume bottles on my dresser. Fluttering over, she picked up my bottle of perfume and turned it over in her hand. "What a pretty bottle, it looks like it's made of a precious gem," she said, twisting the plastic cap. "Is it a potion of some sort?" She jumped a little when the cap popped off, bouncing on the floor.

"Be careful," I said. "It's glass."

She wasn't listening. She tried to unscrew the spray nozzle, and a misty cloud of perfume spritzed her squarely in the face. She screwed up her nose, eyelids fluttering over her slit pupils, as though she were about to sneeze. Dropping the bottle, she started waving her hands in front of her face. "Ah, what is this? A sweet yet foul aura engulfs me! What spell is this, to tickle my nose so?"

"It's called perfume." I knelt and picked up the bottle. "It's just scented water. No more spritzing yourself." I recapped it and put it on the dresser. "You wait here, I need to go and talk to my parents."

"What sort of tome is this?" She had started drifting toward my laptop. "The cover is most intriguing."

"The cover is deceiving," I said, snatching it up and stashing it in a dresser drawer. "It's really a time-wasting device, mostly, and the knowledge it contains is cat videos, and people arguing over politics. Now – try not to touch anything. Especially anything metal." I hesitated before closing the door. "Oh, and no magic. At all. I'm not kidding."

"You are a shower of iron filings upon my joy." Orianna frowned as I closed the door behind me.

I guess that was the Fae version of having your parade rained on. My stomach gave an uncomfortable lurch as I started back down the stairs. My parents had been so grim, yet so close-mouthed. Something told me that this was not going to be about Xandra, or the funeral, or even Orianna. Something else was wrong, and I just didn't know if I could handle even one more problem right now.

8

I hurried down the stairs, hoping against hope that my room would survive that miniature cataclysm that was Orianna. Stepping off the final step, I trod on our new carpeting, still firm yet soft, and reeking of that new-carpet smell. Since Jacquelyn tried to burn our house down, we'd had to completely renovate. Fresh gray paint was on the walls, and Mom had picked out the new dining set from Williams Sonoma.

It had been a double whammy, our house's ruin, coming as it had right after I confessed the secrets I'd been keeping about my life with vampires, werewolves, wizards, and fae. She'd been pretty down, bemoaning the losses until she realized they could remodel the whole first floor with the money we had gotten from the insurance company. That had perked her right up. I guess there really was such a thing as retail therapy.

"I still don't think they'll have anything," Dad said.

"Who'll have anything?" I asked.

They turned and looked at me, the spell of their conversation clearly broken by my entry. "Faerie, huh?" Mom asked. "What's next, leprechauns?"

"Don't jinx it," I said, almost dragging myself into the room. "Unless they bring a big pot of gold with them, big enough to buy me one of those cute Mercedes, a hell of a prom dress, and maybe a shoe-shopping spree at Dolce, I don't really need the trouble they're likely to bring. All I'm saying is, if the reward there is just some Lucky Charms, I'd rather just go to Publix."

"She isn't going to accidentally set the house on fire or anything, is she?" Dad asked, inclining his head toward the upstairs.

"No." I hesitated. "Well...probably not."

Dad rolled his eyes.

"So what's going on?" I asked. The little hairs on the back of my neck were standing up. Not a great sign. Bad things came in threes, didn't they? That was the old adage, I think. I felt it undersold it, really. Mine seemed to appear in dozens. Or grosses, perhaps.

Mom sighed, rubbing her hands over her arms as if she were cold. "Do you remember the private investigators that were looking into my problem?"

An image flashed across my mind of an empty car on the side of the road, of snarling werewolves launching out of the brush at me, blood streaking their coats and muzzles. That had been an unfortunate end for...well, whoever those guys in the Jaguar were. They'd been following me at a most inauspicious time, and paid the price by being eaten by a pack of werewolves. I swallowed nervously. "Yeah?"

"Well, there's a new wrinkle."

"Of course there is," I said, feeling somehow yet more tired. Was tiredness a reserve within me, deep, like magma at my core? Because it felt like it. Cold, tired magma, already cooling to rock, and yearning to wrap itself around me and drag me to bed. "What happened?"

"When we got home, the police were waiting."

"What did they want?"

"They asked some...uncomfortable questions," Dad said. "About the private investigators."

Mom had that distant look in her eyes.

I sat down at the table. "Wait...do they think you're involved with the investigators' death or something?"

Mom pursed her lips, shifting uneasily in her chair.

My stomach twisted into new knots. I wondered if I'd ever have an appetite again.

"It seems that some new evidence has come to light," Dad said.

"What sort of evidence?" I asked. It was frustrating, like pulling teeth to get the information out of them. Couldn't they just tell me? I was already stretched thin as it was.

"They found the records of the PIs' original investigation," Dad said, "and that brought them to your mother."

Mom was pale, and rigid as a wall. Silent was not a good vibe on her.

"What did they find in the records?" I said.

"They didn't really say," Dad said. "And she didn't really answer any of their questions. Pure lawyer, this one."

"I know better than to talk with the police without benefit of counsel," she said. "I set up a time where they could question me with an attorney present."

The cops were involved now. That was bad. Really bad. If anything, anything at all, tied her back to their deaths...

"Thing is, we don't think they know anything," Dad said. "Nothing concrete, at least."

Mom looked at Dad as though he were an idiot. "You cannot possibly believe the detectives put all of their cards on the table. These guys were working a case that involved me right before their deaths. That right there is motive."

I swallowed nervously. Even if it was the werewolves that had killed the investigators, would that matter? How could you explain to the cops, to a coroner, that they'd been devoured by hungry Amish werewolves on a full moon? That didn't feel like a thing that could be penciled in under the cause of death.

And this was all stemming from the original issue with the money that Mom had been borrowing from client accounts. Would they discover that somehow, too?

Where was all of this going to lead?

I was just about to open my mouth to ask another question when there was a scream from upstairs.

I was on my feet and thundering up the stairs at a sprint before it had even begun to fade in the night.

9

I threw myself into my room and was both relieved and startled about what I saw. Iona was standing there, just inside the open window, her face a mask of cold rage. Orianna stood opposite her, flattened against my wall, a glowing orb of golden light in her hand. Iona's teeth were bared, and she was hunched over in a position to leap.

"Wait!" I shouted, jumping between them.

Iona glared at me, fangs distorting her mouth's normal symmetry hideously. "Who is this?"

"Her name is Orianna," I said. "She's a fae."

"I gathered that from the magic and the wings," Iona said, still poised to leap. "You needed my help killing her?"

"What?" My heart jumped. "No! Why would you assume that?"

"Because you called me, of course."

"That's not what–" I sighed heavily. I stood between them, my hands outstretched to hold them back. As if that would help if they decided to attack each other. "She's a–" I started to say "friend." But Orianna wasn't exactly a friend. "I know her," I said, rather lamely. "It's all right."

Iona relaxed a little, but Orianna's hand still glowed with a spell ready to be thrown. What would it do? I didn't know and I didn't care to find out.

"What's going on?" Mom asked. Of course she and Dad had followed me up the stairs.

"It's okay," I said. "Everything's fine. Just a little misunderstanding."

Dad's eyes fell on Iona and the open window behind her. "So, vampires are just letting themselves into our house now? Is it like a vampire drive-through?"

"Yes," Iona said dryly, "this is where I come whenever I want a bite of chicken."

"Dad, it's Iona," I said, like that was more than enough of an explanation, as if she were exempt. Her riposte probably didn't help.

"That does not change the fact that she's a vampire," he said in a more fatherly tone than I had heard him use in a while. He managed to raise his eyes to stare her down. I guess his fatherly instincts had been triggered. Or his manly ones, after being called chicken.

"Iona is not going to eat you," I said. "Tell them, Iona."

"I am probably not going to eat you," Iona said, in a tone that convinced absolutely no one.

Mom gave me a wary and sort of pleading look.

"Iona," I muttered under my breath. "This is not helping."

"Fine," Iona said. "I am definitely not going to eat you...except perhaps in the event of some sort of calamity, like the collapse of society, the end of the blood bank system, or maybe if I find out you do great evil, such as sending Rick Astley links under false pretenses."

"You kill people for Rick-rolling?" my mother asked, her mouth slightly agape.

"She absolutely does not," I said. "She's just terrible with jokes. Now, can I please have the room?"

Mom and Dad shared a glance at me. "Fine," Dad said. "Just...please no more guests without telling us first. And maybe try and avoid ones who'll eat us for rolling a Rick, or whatever it is they just said."

"I also frown on sending links to any song from Dave Matthews Band," Iona called after them. "Just so we're clear on what I kill for."

My dad looked a little offended by that, but they left, blessedly, closing the door behind them.

"What did I say about magic?" I gave Orianna a solid glare.

It faded as she lowered her hand to her side. "My apologies. I felt muchly threatened by this one." She gave Iona a hard look, as if she'd just been sent a Dave Matthews Band link. "Why did you summon this one here, if not to kill me?"

"Because I need her help with myriad other problems," I said. "You know, the ones I was already overwhelmed with before you showed up babbling about summer coming to an end? Which, I mean...hey, I'm all about avoiding that Back-to-School scene, but I'm not sure I can hold back the hands of time."

"That is not...I have no idea what you are talking about," Orianna said.

Iona folded her arms, her amusement – if ever there'd been any – at an end. "So you've got a fae in your room, but you still have other problems besides that?" She paused. "Right. It's you. Of course you do."

I arched my brow at her. "Thanks, and yes, I do. Xandra."

She stared, her face blank. "Yes, I know. Dead girl. What's the problem?"

How was she so dense? "She's not dead anymore," I said.

"Oh?" Iona said, eyebrow cocked. "Oh!...Oh." It was a whole emotional progression, the five stages crammed into one word, spoken three times. "They turned her?"

"Yes," I said, "because they're evil and hate me. How did you not see this coming?"

"Because I'm not evil and I don't hate you, I suppose," Iona said. "Still, though, ace move by Jacquelyn, given her life goal is making yours an absolute nightmare. Well played on her part."

"Who is Jackie-lynn?" Orianna said.

"Vampire," I said, off handed.

"Oh dear, you have vampire enemies and friends?" Orianna asked. "How do you tell them apart?"

I was too tired to probe that further, but Iona glared at her, then moved to my bed. She sat on the edge, staring up at me. "Sorry that you had to deal with that alone. If you suspected it, why didn't you ask me to stay in case it happened?"

"I was wallowing in misery," I said. "And I wasn't positive it was going to happen."

"And here I thought misery loved company," Iona said.

"In my case," I said, "misery prefers to be alone, because company might try and talk me into feeling better when I'd really rather feel worse."

"Very healthy," Iona said. She shifted her arms uncomfortably, staring at the floor. "So was she hostile? Because that's normal. When you come out of the grave, you're disoriented. It's a tough time."

I didn't want to hope for anything, but I asked, "Does that mean that she could still, like...turn out okay?"

Iona looked up at me with her sad, pale eyes. "I don't want to say anything, Cassie. Just in case things don't turn out well. It depends. On a lot of things." I closed my mouth, the questions that had sprung up in my mind fading. "There is no guarantee, not in either direction."

"According to her," I said. "she remembered everything. And it was like she hated me the way Jacquelyn does. Like she blamed me for what happened."

"I am lost. What happened?" Orianna asked.

"My best friend was turned, obviously," I said.

Orianna nodded. "Ah, I see. Turned how?"

"Into a vampire," I said. I was starting to lose my patience with her.

Orianna's slitted pupils were partially covered by her gold-shaded eyelids. "This is all very strange."

"So are you," Iona said.

Orianna's hair started to swell, her eyes narrowing.

"Easy," I said.

Iona kept her attention to me. "So what happened after she came out of the grave? Did she attack you?"

"Yep."

"And I saved her," Orianna said brightly, beaming at me.

"She...I don't know if she was trying to kill me, but she definitely was not trying to be gentle." I rubbed at my neck again. "I don't know what to do now. I'm worried Jacquelyn is going to seek her out."

Iona shrugged. "Kindred spirits? Maybe."

My stomach did a flip at the thought of two of my former best friends hating me in alliance. "Oh, no."

"Don't get down yet," Iona said. "There's no way to know for sure what she'll do."

So there was hope. Albeit a very small amount, there was hope. "After Orianna knocked her away from me, she took off. I have no idea where she went. Lockwood and I drove around looking for her, but couldn't find her."

"Well, when you first come out, you look for familiar

ground," Iona said. "It's a comfort thing, almost instinctual. She'll want to seek somewhere her memories have held onto, somewhere she'll remember immediately."

I wanted to ask her more about what her experience was like, but could tell by her bearing that she did not want to talk about it. "Lockwood and I checked at her house," I said. "But she wasn't there."

Iona shook her head. "Probably wouldn't go there. Her parents are there, and with the state she's in, her dawning awareness, she'll know that and she won't want to see them."

"Really?" I said. "Is that why she was so upset to see me?"

She didn't answer that. Just stared at me, then past me, remembering. "The thirst doesn't come on right away. She's going to avoid people for the moment. Like I said, disoriented. She's going to have to come to terms with what happened."

"Familiar ground..." I said, starting to pace across my room. Not that there was much room to do that, with two other people in here. "Where would she go where there are no people?"

"What about the mall?" Iona said. "It's the middle of the night, big space, no one would be there."

"No, she hated the mall. Familiar, but unoccupied..." I stopped mid-pace, my eyes falling on a picture of her and me during lunch, sitting out at our favorite table outside of the cafeteria. "Summer's not over," I said, prompting Orianna to look at me quizzically. "School, Orianna, not your problem, whatever it is. School's out – and if I were looking for a place to be alone...that's where I'd go."

10

The high school sat silent, foreboding, and slightly spotted through the front windshield of Iona's old but scrupulously maintained Volkswagen Beetle. It hummed surprisingly smoothly for such an old car, Iona sullenly at the wheel, me staring out the window of the passenger side and Orianna...

Well, Orianna was in the back, face pressed against the window like a Garfield cat, apparently enjoying the sensation of being squired in a horseless carriage.

"What about her favorite restaurant?" Iona asked as we pulled into the parking lot. "Or park? Did she like the beach?"

"Why are you so determined that it wouldn't be the school?" I said, scanning the front of the building for lights, broken windows, busted doors, my best friend the vampire leering out of the darkness surrounded by bats. A sign, really.

Iona huffed through her nose and spoke nearly under her breath. "I am not going to argue with you because you have recently been through a tragedy. All the social etiquette books I've read have said to give your friends in those times comfort and an '*ear to listen*'. Even if you are wrong."

"Wait," I said, trying to process that. "You read etiquette books? Was that a part of your ancient upbringing?"

"They were modern," Iona said, suddenly shifting very uncomfortably in her seat.

"Did you..." I felt a weird, amusing, squirming sensation inside. "...did you read those books just for me?"

"I did not read–" she started, and then deflated. "Okay, yeah, I totally read those for you." She shifted uncomfortably in the driver's seat, avoiding my eye. "It was pointed out by Forehead that I needed to soften my approach with you. Apparently I was too brash."

"You and Mill had conversations when I wasn't around?" The mind boggled.

She glared. "I do have a life outside of you, you know. Also, we were stuck in a trunk for a very long time on our way to New York. Even I can't keep quiet for that long."

"You travel in a trunk?" Orianna asked, still pressed to the window. She'd gone quite mad when we'd passed the lighted sign at Burger King. "An odd way to travel, secreting yourself away in luggage. It must have been a very large case."

"I'm gonna need a case of something to deal with the wide-eyed Princess of Aurium back there," Iona said under her breath. But without breath. "What is it she needs from you, exactly, and how soon could we be rid of her if we really focused on it?"

"I don't know," I said. "Something about Faerie falling apart, Summer diminishing, Winter filling the breach. It didn't sound like light work, the sort of thing you can fix in a break between classes."

Iona's eyes widened. "What kind of problems are they having that require you?"

"Clearly very serious ones if they're seeking me out," I said with a shrug. "Hey, slow down here." We were rolling past the science wing, and Iona was not sparing the minuscule horsepower available to her.

"What does Lockwood think of this?" Iona said, tapping the brakes.

"He's not thrilled," I said. "He and Orianna don't exactly get along."

"And I don't understand why," Orianna said, her golden eyes narrowing, lips turning in a frown. "I thought we were getting along splendidly before he was banned from Faerie."

"Stop here," I said as we rolled past the front door. Iona did, and I peered at it. The light overhead was out, and long shadows swept over the facade and covered the front stairs. Even still...

...I could tell from here the front door was cracked open.

"I hate being right," I muttered, mostly to myself.

Orianna did not take it that way, though. "Really?" she chirped. "I love being right. Especially when I can take that fact and rub people's noses in it like unicorn dung, so very 'Take that! Enjoy the sniff of my rightness, like unicorn dung upon your face! Ha!'" And she clapped. Like an idiot.

"If all the Fae are like her," Iona said, deadpan, "I can see why they need your help."

But I was too busy thinking about the immediate problem, the open door to the school. Which might just mean my dead best friend was hiding inside.

Gulp.

11

"Listen, no one hates to be right," Iona said as she killed the ignition. It sputtered and clanged, then silence fell over us, and I could hear a low ringing in my ears. "People love to be right more than they love breathing."

"Love breeding?" Orianna said. "Humans love breeding?"

I froze rather awkwardly. "Uhm. Um."

"Don't faeries?" Iona said.

"I certainly don't." Orianna shuddered. "It's icky, and when you're done, there's glitter everywhere, I hear. No, no. Not for me."

"Well, I said 'breathing.'" Iona said.

"Which was an odd choice," I said, opening the door, "considering you don't breathe."

"Yes," Iona said, getting out. She leaned on the top of the car, staring over it at the front of the school. "And I do miss it sometimes."

"Why?" I asked, genuinely perplexed. "When you exert yourself as a human, you sound like you're gasping. Ten minutes of cardio and it's like I'm dying. But you can lift a car, run ten miles, and you're still quiet like a stealth bomber. There's a lot of things I would not like about vampirism, but that's not one of them."

Iona made a grunt of pure frustration. "I just mean that people would rather die than be wrong."

"No," I said, looking out at the open door. That cool breeze came through again, pushing it gently open, making it squeal on its hinges. That was eerie. "I would definitely rather I was wrong in this situation."

"Hey, wait for me," Orianna said, thumping her palm against the door. Before I had a chance to help her, there was a blast of golden light, and the door flew open.

"Hey, if you broke anything – " Iona started.

Orianna cast another ball of golden light at the car, but the door slid shut with a *click* that said that it was, indeed, closed. "I think I'm getting the hang of these human devices," she said with an annoying amount of pride.

I sighed, looking around. "If she's in there, we shouldn't go in blind."

"Well," Iona said, "since you hate breathing so much, I'm surprised you don't love being blind, too. I mean, is there any part of the human condition you feel tied to?"

"Are you taking this personally?" I asked, feeling a little weird. "I was just saying–"

"It doesn't matter right now," Iona said huffily. "You want to know what's going on here? Send her." She pointed at Orianna.

I looked at Orianna. It wasn't a bad idea. "Since you're here, would you be willing to help us out?"

Orianna perked up. It was almost as if I could still see her wings lifting at the same time her eyebrows did. "Of course. Anything you need. I would be pleased to indebt you further to me."

I cringed. Damned Fae and their webs of obligation. "Would you mind doing a quick fly around, see if anyone's in the area?"

She hopped into the air, and grinned down at me. "Certainly. I'll be right back." My heart was uneasy as we watched her hover higher and higher, disappearing around the perimeter of the building.

"Why are you accumulating these winged people?" Iona asked the moment she was gone.

I looked over at her. "I'll make sure to tell Lockwood what you called him."

She arched an eyebrow at me.

"Honestly, I don't know," I said, waiting for her to reappear. "Why do vampires keep showing up for me?"

Iona made a derisive noise, blowing air through her lips. "Because you've meddled in vampire affairs. And survived. One of those is rarer than the other. Personally, I would have suggested cutting your losses and moving, but according to this advice column I consulted, I'd be overstepping by suggesting that."

"Did you write a Dear Abby letter?"

"It was *Cosmo*'s advice column, actually," she said a bit snippily.

"Hmmm," I said. "Well, look on the bright side. If I hadn't meddled, we might never have met. And you'd have missed out on sleepovers and braiding each other's hair."

Iona subconsciously ran her fingers through her hair, running them over a thin braid that was tied with a red ribbon at the end. "All I am saying is that you can't go blaming vampires for the choices you've made, Cassandra." My nose wrinkled at the sound of my full name. "Most of us were more than happy to leave you alone, but you keep sticking your nose in our business."

"Thanks, *Mom*," I said, glaring at her. "What is up with you? Are you arguing on Varycas's behalf now?"

She seemed a little taken aback by that, tossing her hair over her shoulder. "No, but I do see his point...which is that you could have walked away from this multiple times. After Byron died, for instance. After you killed those Instaphoto vampires."

"Not easily," I said. "Draven kind of did all he could to get my attention. Or to put it the way my dad and Mill did, 'Just when I thought I was out, they pull me back in.'"

Iona stared at me blankly. "What is that? Is that a quote from something?"

"I don't know, either," I gushed. "But they were very excited about it. They were like me and Xandra going on about the new cupcakes flavors at Gigi's."

Iona's eyes fluttered and narrowed, unable to conceal her annoyance at my food reference. "Whatever the case, the many opportunities for you to stay out of vampire affairs. You passed on all of them."

"Like what?" I asked. "Letting Laura get killed by the Instaphoto vamps? Letting my town in New York just go down to the vampire problems I brought to their door?"

"It wouldn't have been your fault," Iona said.

"Pretty sure that one would have been truly my fault," I said. "Draven sent the Butcher there looking for me. That's my fault, my responsibility."

"No, it's not," Iona said. "You take all of this so person-ally, think that it's somehow your responsibility to fix it all. Draven was sending the Butcher as a deterrent. You'd attacked his territory twice. Okay, fine. You want to talk about consequences? There's your consequences. Take your

lumps and move on with your human life. Instead, you esca-
lated at every turn, involving yourself deeper in our world.
Jacquelyn was born from that. Then you stuck your nose in
Faerie–"

"I did not! Lockwood dragged me over there against my
will!" I opened my mouth to argue, but stopped. "You are
right, though. I could have walked away multiple times. But
I just can't quit you people now."

Her glare hardened. "Are you mocking me?"

"No," I said. "Not right this moment, anyway. I really
meant it. It's kind of hard to walk away from vampire affairs
now that my best friend is apparently one of you."

Before she could respond, a flicker of gold above us
caught my eye, and I looked up to see Orianna floating
down to us. "Nobody is in the area," she said. "And there are
no other doors open on this strange castle."

"...Castle?" I looked over the front of the school. "Okay. I
can sort of see it, I guess. If it was dark. And I squinted."

"What lord lives here?" Orianna asked.

"It's summer, so no one right now," I said, taking halting
steps toward the wide-open front door. "But from autumn to
spring, it's the Lord of 'Edu-cay-shun.'"

"He sounds terrifying," Orianna said, clamping a gold-
covered hand over her mouth.

"Oh, he is," I said with great seriousness as Iona smol-
dered. "He is brutal and distributes many detentions to the
subjects that do not follow the laws of his land."

"These detentions sound painful," Orianna said. "What
is detained? Eyes? Entrails?"

"All," I said. "Come on, let's go." And I gripped the front
door, ready to embrace a trespassing charge. Hopefully
Mom would be able to get me off if the cops caught me...as-
suming she wasn't disbarred.

"Was it worse than the time we were in captivity and at the mercy of the Summer Court?" Orianna asked, fluttering into the darkened hallway behind me.

I considered for a second. "You know, if it's Miss Reynolds, then yeah, I think it's worse than that." I stopped just inside. Other than the glint of a few stray colored LEDs as part of the fire system, I couldn't see anything, and I said so.

"No problem," Orianna said. With a little flutter of her hand, it was as if I were staring into the building in the middle of the day.

I blinked a few times, but I could still see clearly. "How did you...?"

"Less conspicuous than a ball of floating light, right?" Orianna said.

The lobby was just like it always was. The school's banner hung from the second-floor landing, reminding us to have school pride and support our sports teams. The trophy cabinets that housed the various minor and ultimately meaningless accomplishments of students through the years were untouched. The only sound was a soft *tick tock* from the clock on the wall, reminding me that it was well past my bedtime. As if my sagging eyelids weren't doing that already.

We stepped inside, walking as quietly as we could. My dress shoes *clacked* a little more than I would have liked in the large, echoing room, but Iona was completely silent. Orianna was hovering just above the ground, the whip of her wings subtle as a bee's.

I looked around this quiet room and thought...maybe someone just forgot to close the front door?

But no. That was not likely.

I licked my lips, listening hard for the scrape of a chair,

or the slam of a door. But all I could hear was the thud of my own blood against my eardrum.

Where would she go? The school was huge, and there were plenty of places she would be familiar with. She'd avoid the gym at all costs; she hated Mrs. Lawrence. I was pretty certain she'd never set foot in the music wing. And while she might have thought the new Bio teacher was super hot, she'd almost failed the class. Not a familiar feeling for Xandra. The lunchroom was a viable option, but we sat outside more than we ever did inside, and Orianna had already said no one was out there.

I got so tired of my shoes clacking against the floor that I pulled them off, choosing to go barefoot. I didn't want to think about how long it had been since the janitors had probably deep cleaned the place, but hey, at least I was moving as silently as someone with a heartbeat could.

We turned a corner, and I saw the row of lockers where Xandra and I would talk in the mornings before homeroom. It was strange. That life didn't really feel like mine. It was like I was watching a movie of someone else's, or maybe read a really vivid story that just made it seem like my life, if only for a moment. The memory faded as I peered into the open door of our English class.

How was it that I was standing at her grave just a few hours ago? I could still see the shifting dirt, hear her croaking voice as she stared up at me from the churning earth. The tear stains were still sticky on my cheeks. Heartache threatened to overwhelm me.

Moonlight was spilling in through the windows on the far wall. The desks were in perfect rows. The chalkboard was blank. The teacher's desk at the front was uncluttered; it was a room in the throes of summer, nigh abandoned.

Nigh. Meaning "nearly."

Because there she was, sitting at her old desk beside the windows, second to last in the row, the moonlight making her periwinkle hair look as if it were glowing.

My heart clenched in my chest to see her again. I had hoped that somehow tiredness had caused me to hallucinate the last few hours. That really, her grave was still full and undisturbed, wet with the midnight dew.

But she was sitting there like it was a normal day at school, as if waiting patiently for the teacher to arrive, the students to fill in the desks around her. The bell would ring any second. Class would commence with notes scrawled on the board for us to copy.

She was just sitting there, perfectly still, staring off into space, her hands folded daintily on the desk in front of her.

There was no rise and fall of her chest.

And that's when I realized...

The Xandra that I knew...the Xandra that was my best friend...

Was truly dead and gone.

12

I stepped into the room, and quickly realized that was a pretty poor idea. The tile under my foot made scarcely a sound, but it instantly drew Xandra's attention over to us at the door. "Uh oh," I said.

Xandra was on her feet in one fluid motion, far more gracefully than I had ever seen her leave a desk. Her stature transformed from that of a school girl to a she-beast. Her jaw split and her teeth were bared. She hunched her shoulders like a cat and extended her hands as if ready to claw at us. A low, deep growl passed between her lips, and my blood ran cold.

A thin arm came down like a barrier before me. "You don't want any part of this, she's not herself," Iona said, stepping in front of me. "The beast has her." She flexed her fingers, readying her stance.

Then she shoved me out of the way, back into the hall. I floundered on my feet for a second, trying to catch my balance. The door slammed, and I scrambled back to the window to see what was happening.

It was like a tornado had been loosed in the English

class. Xandra had thrown herself at Iona, knocking the metal and plywood desks out of her way as if they were made of flimsy cardboard. Iona caught her, and they spun in a balletic dance, more force being exerted on either side than I could have mustered in a lifetime.

"Xandra, it's me," I said, peering through the window as two vampires battled. I wasn't even sure why I was trying. How could she hear me over the sound of screeching metal chairs on the tile floor? "We're here to help you. Just give us a second to–"

Orianna grabbed me out of the way as the two vampires crashed through the cinderblock wall. A shower of dust and the crash of broken concrete echoed through the halls. The two of them were rolling across the tile before they slammed into the lockers on the opposite wall, leaving a five-foot indent in the metal. Iona had her against the lockers, teeth bared.

But Xandra was not just taking it. Her fangs were out, fully extended, her eyes narrowed, almost completely black with rage.

For a moment, it was as if I were staring into the face of Theo again as he tried to corner me like the little lamb I was back then. That look so common to vampires, blood-hungry, fangs out, terrifying, was now upon a face I would never have wished to see it on, not ever.

Without really thinking, I pulled the stake from my hair. My defenses were up, I was warring with myself.

It was Xandra.

But it was *not* Xandra.

There was a yelp of pain, and they both were flung back from each other with a bang against the metal.

Iona grabbed at her arm. Black blood oozed between her fingers. Xandra had landed a blow with her newfound claws. They surged together again, forces of nature unleashed in the E Wing hallway. The collision was loud, made me flinch.

With one swift motion, Iona lifted Xandra into the air and tossed her farther down the hall. She banged off the lockers, but landed easily on her feet, catlike reflexes coming to her rescue. She hissed, glaring down the hall...

And then...she was gone. A flash of shadow, a hint of purple, and the skitter of her footsteps as she broke into flight. Iona took off after her, silvery hair streaming behind her as she rounded the corner. No breath, just the dull of quick footsteps as the chase was on.

I followed after, though much slower. Orianna kept pace with me, flying beside me even though she could have easily outstripped me. Rounding a corner, I saw Xandra and Iona at the very end of the long hall. Xandra was at full sprint, Iona nearly on her tail.

Xandra slammed into the emergency exit door, charging through it without stopping, the metal parting and crashing into the brick walls on either side. Iona followed wordlessly, a low growl trailing her.

I was gasping for breath by the time that Orianna and I reached the open door. Stepping out into the cool night, I panted in the chill air, looking around.

They were nowhere in sight. I wiped my forehead with the back of my hand and stared around.

"Wasn't the blonde one carrying those?" Orianna said, flitting down beside me, wings glinting in the lamplight.

"What?" I saw her pointing to the ground just outside of the doors. Something silver shone on the concrete. I knelt and picked up Iona's car keys. They clinked in my grasp.

Clever girl. Dropped them so we didn't have to walk. Besides, there was no way we were going to catch two vampires at a full run. Even Orianna would have trouble keeping up with them.

"They're gone," Orianna said, buzzing up ten feet and peering into the distance. A chain-link fence lay just ahead, clinking as if the wind had got hold of it.

"Yeah. They must have hopped the fence." I slid my finger through the keyring and clasped the keys tightly in my palm. A dress meant no pockets.

"So...what do we do now?" Orianna said, buzzing back down to me. Her golden eyes gleamed with curiosity, waiting for my answer.

"Well," I said. "There's no point waiting for them here." In the distance, I heard a siren. Headed our way? I didn't want to find out. "Come on. Let's get out of here."

13

"So," Orianna said, once we were in motion, "since we didn't catch that girl, could we maybe talk about what I need now?" Her voice was hesitant, as if she expected me to explode.

I flipped the turn signal on Iona's bug, taking us down a street a couple over from the school, and sighed. "Sure. Unless Iona catches her, there's nothing I can do about Xandra for the time being. Why don't you burden me with even more problems?"

"Perfect." Orianna opened her mouth, then snapped it shut. "Wait. Was that human sarcasm?"

"Yes," I said, "but go ahead anyway." I fought back a yawn.

Orianna took a deep breath. "I told you that the Winter Court was growing stronger, trying to compensate for the diminishment of Summer?" She stole a nervous glance out the window. "Well, it's starting to bleed over onto Earth."

"What do you mean, bleed over?" I said, keeping a hand on the bug's wheel and my speed steady so I didn't have to shift. Stupid manual transmission. I could drive it, unlike so many of my peers, but I didn't like it.

"There are wards between Faerie and Earth," Orianna said. "Designed to prevent our magic from leaking over into your – excuse me for saying so, prosaic, boring world." I gave her a look; she did not notice. "But something has happened that has made the wards weaker. Some have broken all together. So parts of Earth are coming through to Faerie, and vice versa."

"Okay," I said. "What does that mean for us, though?"

"I don't know, exactly," Orianna said, cocking her head curiously. "But I have been told by those wiser than me–" I barely kept my eyelid from twitching and my mouth from spitting out, "So, literally everyone?" Instead I just kept listening to her, "–that Faerie's magic pouring over into Earth is 'not good,' and that something must be done about it."

"But you only mentioned Winter," I said. "You don't know what's causing Summer's diminishment? At all?"

"No one does," she said. "At least not among the Unseelie. It is a great mystery."

"All right." I glanced over at her. "I still don't understand why you need me."

Orianna shifted uncomfortably in her seat. "I thought that much was obvious."

"Maybe I'm just tired, but...no. Nothing is obvious. Not to me." The Beetle shuddered as I coaxed it into a turn. "Not right now."

"I was the one who suggested we reach out to you," Orianna said, beaming. "Because whatever is going in, it is happening in your world, see?"

"I...not really," I said. "Wait. Am I the only human you know?"

"You are the only human that most people in our court have ever laid eyes on," Orianna said.

"What about Lockwood?" I said.

Orianna shook her head, and I could have sworn that I heard a faint tinkling of bells. "He was Summer Court."

I shook my head. These Fae and their ideas of clannishness. "I can kind of see why he left," I muttered.

Orianna nodded her head, a sad look passing over her face. "Yes. No one would want to live in a world of iron unless they had a compelling motivation for doing so. I honestly do not know how he stands it." She ran her fingers delicately over the Beetle's window. "It's all so...strange."

"Yeah, well, I thought the same about Faerie. Magic is cool and all, but I am totally fine not having to live with it day to day."

"And I can't imagine living in a world without it." She smiled a little sadly. "We are so different, aren't we?"

"Indeed," I said. "So what do you want me to do, exactly?"

"Well," Orianna said, "I was wondering if you had any ideas."

"No, of course I don't," I said, frowning. "I only know of two faeries in my world; Lockwood and this other creepy one that dabbles in blood magic."

"Oh, we don't want him," Orianna said, wrinkling her nose.

"No one wants him," I said.

There was a part of me that wondered if Orianna wasn't being completely forthcoming with what she wanted. I kept this thought to myself, though. The only other thing I could think that they might want from me was my ability to see through glamours. How that squared with Orianna's explanation...well, I just couldn't see it.

We were a quarter mile from making the turn onto my street when we passed by a gas station, and I recognized the car filling up there. It was a dark green Honda Civic, and standing beside it was Derrick Bauer, half asleep under the gas station lights as he watched the numbers tick up. Without hesitating, I pulled into the station and parked right behind him.

"What are we doing?" Orianna said. "This does not look like the tower you call home."

"Just hold on a second," I said. "Stay in here." I popped open the door and called, "Hey, Derrick," into the night.

Derrick jumped, almost into the air. Then he wheeled around, staring at me with wide, pale blue eyes. "Cassie," he said once he'd come back down. "Hey." He relaxed...but only a little.

I leaned against Iona's car, folding my arms across my chest. One of the lights overhead was flickering, while the others bathed us both in a sickly yellow light. "You're out kind of late."

His face paled. "I could say the same about you."

My eyes narrowed. "I hang out with the vampire set, remember?"

Derrick scratched at the back of his head. "Right, yeah." The pump gave a loud *thunk* indicating that it was full, and I thought he was going to jump out of his skin.

"So what's up with you and Jed?" I asked, too tired to be subtle.

"What do you mean?" He fumbled with the pump as he pulled it from the car, accidentally dribbling a half gallon of precious unleaded all over the concrete. "There's nothing going on." He wasn't making eye contact, either.

"Right," I said, my eyes narrowing. "Sure."

He shrugged. "Well, hey, nice running into you, but if I

don't get home, my mom is going to wonder where I am and I promised I'd be back by–" He glanced at his watch. "Now, actually. See you later, okay?" He pulled open his door and slid inside with a little wave, then proceeded to turn his car on.

I waved back as he drove past and turned back out onto the road. When I slid into the driver's seat, Orianna was peering out of the window in the direction he had driven off.

"Anything about that seem funny to you?" I asked her as I turned the car back on. I stared straight out the window into the night as the air came on, chilly, and I shut it off. The gas station light flickered again overhead.

"That boy is lying to you," she said, her glow lighting the interior of the Beetle. Orianna was almost smiling, but sadly. "Take it from one who knows."

And I knew, as I put the car in gear...in this, at least, she was telling the truth.

14

"Back so soon?" Mom asked as Orianna and I came in through the back door of my house. We'd given up after a half hour or so of searching for Iona and Xandra. They'd vanished into the night, and my eyelids were getting too heavy to continue. Reluctantly, I'd steered us toward home. I wiped my sweaty hands on my sweaty dress, the hem all wrinkled and spotted with dirt from the cemetery.

Mom frowned, probably imagining the laundry nightmare she'd be dealing with cleaning it later. "So, did you do what you set out to do?"

"No," I said.

"Okay. What did you set out to do?" Dad asked.

"I don't need to know," Mom said, pulling a file in front of her. The table was piled with them. Was this what adults did? Had conversations about insurance, and examined files? Honestly, after my night, it sounded...calming. "Not sure I want to know, either."

"Yeah, but you probably should know." I took a deep breath, exhaling through my nose. "It's about Xandra. She... well, I found out that she..."

"Is...everything okay?" Dad said.

"There's no easy way to say this," I said, holding my hands out in exasperation. "Xandra is...a vampire now."

Mom looked very steadily at me, as if trying to decide something. "Is everyone a vampire in your world at this point, sweetie? Are *we* vampires?"

I glared at her. "Well, you are a blood sucking lawyer, so...maybe?"

Dad put a hand on Mom's arm, stopping her from spitting out the retort on her tongue. "Honey, I think she's serious."

"I am fully serious," I said, and gave a quick account of what happened at the cemetery, followed by the chase at the school. I was surprised that neither of them seemed surprised that the school had been wrecked in Iona and Xandra's fight. The shock of Xandra coming back from the grave seemed to overshadow all that.

"So, now what?" Mom said, leaning back in her chair. Dad had risen and put the teapot on to boil. I watched longingly as he pulled the box of chamomile down from the cupboard.

"I'm not really sure," I said. "Iona has to catch her, I guess. But I don't know what happens after that. I don't have much experience with fledgling vampires. Most of my dealings with vamps are of the," and I mimed a stabbing motion, "ugh, gurk! variety."

It was weird to think of Xandra in that context. Like I'd have to stake her.

"I'm sorry, Cass," Dad said, pouring some of the water into some mugs. "I can't imagine what you're going through right now.

Orianna sniffed at the hot liquid in the mug before her.

She was just about to drink it before I put my hand between her mouth and the mug. "Don't. Let it steep."

She frowned at me, lowering the mug. "Speaking of steep, perhaps you can clear something up for me."

"Like what?" I said.

"Okay, so this Xandra, she *was* your best friend." Orianna looked at me with those weird pupils. "So...who is your best friend *now?*"

I saw Mom arch a brow out of the corner of my eye, probably reflecting the same look on my face. "I don't really know what you mean."

"Would it be that Derrick person we ran into at the place with the bright lights and the tubes that fed the metal beasts? The place with the funny smells?"

I looked at her, my brow furrowing. "You mean the gas station...?"

Orianna was staring at me in great concentration. "Is it a hierarchy, where someone moves up when the previous best friend dies?"

I rubbed my forehead. "Why, are you trying to figure out how to slide into the top spot?"

"You ran into Derrick tonight?" Mom said, clutching her steaming mug between her hands. "Isn't that the boy who's the son of that werewolf?" She paused, and nearly shuddered. "Werewolves, faeries, vampires, witches...what has happened to you, Cassandra?"

"I gave up lying and started killing vampires," I said, the drag of tiredness threatening to pull me down. I could go to sleep right here on the rug. "What do you want from me?"

"I think I preferred the lying," Mom said under her breath.

"No, you did not," I said.

"The lying was so much more real than faeries and

vampires and all this," she said, gesturing around the room, mostly in Orianna's general direction.

There was a knock at the door, and all four of us turned toward it. Mom and Dad's eyes fell on me.

I absorbed their looks, but felt a bit put out by it. "What? Like your friends are too good to show up for a visit in the middle of the night."

Before I get up and answer it, the door swung open, and in strolled Iona. She tossed her very wind-blown hair over her shoulder, and there was black blood clinging to her skin and clothes like she'd rolled around in a slick of oil. She gave me a very nonplussed look and announced, "I lost her."

"Are we not locking the door now?" Dad asked. "It feels like, given everything that's going on, we should be locking the door."

An angry wound on Iona's arm had caught my eye, still weeping oily black, and there was an ebon stain on her white shirt just above her hip. She sagged against the counter, holding the bloody spot at her side. "I'm not sure what kind of conversation you two had at her graveside," she said. "But she is *mad*. Madder even than usual for a brand-new fledgling. She tore me right open." With a smack of her lips and a surprising amount of calm, she asked, "Do you have any blood?"

"Hello, Iona," Dad said with a little wave that just oozed defeat. Mom stroked her neck, protectively.

"No I don't," I answered her. "Do you really need any more blood?"

She winced a little. "Well, if I don't have to run any more marathons, I should be okay. I am thirsty, though."

Mom gave me a very pointed look. "Can I get you some water?" she asked, moving toward the faucet. "Tea?"

"Not unless you want me to spew black bile all over your

lovely home," Iona said. Mom immediately turned off the faucet.

"So where's Xandra headed" I asked.

"I don't know," Iona said. "She's been driven off her chosen home ground. So now it is likely she is going to run into an unfamiliar place." She grimaced, probing at the wound at her side. "The blood lust is starting to waken in her."

A chill swept through the room as the humans realized what she was describing. Hello, anxiety, my old friend. My stomach twisted in knots as I looked down at the floor. Mom had some new tile laid when the house was renovated. It looked like wood. It was still perfect, looked as good as the day it was installed.

"That said," Iona went on, "I did manage to scratch her enough that she'll probably hunker down for the night, wherever she ends up."

"Is that a guarantee?" I asked.

Iona shook her head. "You should know by now...there are no guarantees."

I pinched the bridge of my nose, my head giving an angry, sudden throb. All of this pent-up stress had to go somewhere, didn't it? It's too bad that I didn't have one of Varycas's minions around. I could really do with shoving my stake through something. I looked at the clock over the stove. "It's late," I said, more for the benefit of myself than of the others. "There shouldn't be too many people out for Xandra to run into."

"We better hope not," Iona said. "She might not be able to control herself if she gets a whiff of – well. You know."

"Carne asada?" My dad said oh-so-helpfully. "I know I have real problems resisting a taco truck when I smell one."

No one laughed, except Orianna, who probably did not know what a taco even was.

I kept quiet, I kept calm, at least on the outside. The idea of Xandra killing some random person was enough to make me want to push the fae beside me out the front window. That wasn't just because she'd been following me around all night, though. Orianna was rocking back and forth on her heels, even though she wasn't even on the ground at all. I watched her for a few seconds, then said, "You look like you are just about to burst. What are you thinking?"

Orianna's eyes widened as she floated over to me. "So...are you going to do anything about this tonight? Or can we do something for me?"

I narrowed my eyes. "Is this why you were asking about a hierarchy of best friends? If you make it in, you think I'll help you?"

"Okay, well, I'm out," Mom said, throwing up her hands. "My dinette is Grand Central Station with vampires and faeries." She threw down the file she'd been clutching, pushed away her tea, and stood up. "Also, my eyes are blurring and I can't read. Everyone have a wonderful night, please try not to get killed or..." and she looked at Iona, "...kill anyone." With that, she headed for the stairs.

"Night, Mom," I called after her.

"Good night, Cassandra's mother!" Orianna called after her. "Sleep in peace, awaken refreshed and with renewed life."

"I should go to bed, too," Dad said, eyeing Orianna. "She's a bit...stressed."

"I gathered that," I said.

He hesitated before following her up, turning back to me. "If you do go back out to look for Xandra, just be careful? And call if you need anything." He disappeared up the stairs, soft footsteps as my father receded from me.

My heart ached a little, and I shoved the sentimentality away. I had enough to feel right now. I turned back to Orianna. "What do you want me to do?"

Orianna blinked innocently. "...Hm? To have your help, of course?"

"My help is not currently helpful," I said. "I'm tired, I'm crabby, everything is falling apart around me. Other than one Seelie who is my friend–"

"Yes, let's leave him out of this, please," Orianna said.

"–I have little to offer you," I said. "And I have no energy for lies or games. So...what. Do you. Want. Me. To do?"

"Well," she said coyly, "I do have one thing. A contact that would have been my first stop if finding you or convincing you to help me didn't pan out. One of the ex-pats that left Faerie. The Court gave me their location."

"Why didn't you talk to this contact first?" I said. "It sure would have made my life easier."

"It would have made it shorter, certainly," she said with a haughtily arched eyebrow. "I saved you, after all. Anyhow, this contact would be one I could go to for information, but not someone the Court trusts to resolve the situation."

I looked to Iona. "If we are about to go traipsing through the city, do you wanna go grab some blood at home? Or do you want to come and talk to some Winter ex-pat with me?"

Iona looked at me hard. "Where?"

I turned my attention back to Orianna for explanation. "It's a place called *Coldsnap*," she said.

"Please tell me that it's not like in California or something," I said, the exhaustion washing over me again, making all my limbs feel like lead.

"No, it's in Tampa," Iona said, and I must have given her

a funny look. "They made me stand outside for three hours once," she added. "In the sweaty night heat."

"'Sweaty night heat?'" Orianna asked, her voice taking on a dreamlike quality. "That sounds just *terrible*."

"It was," Iona said, giving her an odd look.

I massaged my temples. "Why is *everything* monster-related in Tampa? Are these franchise opportunities?"

"This is just the only city where you're aware of beings thought to be myths," Iona said. "You went to Miami, and New York and found vampires both places."

"So can we go to this place of sweaty night heat?" Orianna said, clasping her hands together tightly underneath her chin, her golden eyes like a doe's shining at me.

"Please never describe it that way again," I said, "and yes. I suppose."

"Fine." Iona rolled her eyes. "I'll come."

That was a bolt out of the blue. "You sure?" I asked, eyeing her wound, which she was currently trying to staunch with paper towels. "Maybe it'd be better if you, y'know…"

"Healed from the last grievous wounding you gave me?" Iona asked. "I think we both know the opportunities for that are a bit thin on the ground when I go for a night out with you." She patted herself with a black-soaked paper towel. "I'll have to improvise. Got any duct tape?"

"Yeah, I'm sure Dad has some," I said. "I'll change, grab a stake or two, some duct tape, and we'll go." I made a face. "That sounded like a creep-o's shopping list. Maybe Mom's right about me changing for the worst. At least the lies were kind of normal."

"Don't forget a jacket," Iona called up after me. "It's getting a bit chilly out there."

I pulled on some shorts and a T-shirt, then the jacket

Iona suggested. And just for safe keeping, I grabbed a silver-tipped stake that Lockwood had made for me. My hands hovered over a little wooden box right beside my spare stakes. I pocketed that, too.

No point in being unprepared.

15

"So, Coldsnap," I said as Iona pulled into an empty spot along the curb. "That's clever for the middle of Tampa. Ironic or whatever."

"Yes, they're real hipsters, these Winter Fae," Iona said acidly. She wore a perpetual cringe and, for once, I suspected it was based on genuine pain rather than a generalized loathing for the world and nearly everyone in it. She had a true commitment to her misanthropic tendencies, and I respected that.

I looked out of the windshield up the street. We were in what looked to be a section of town populated by old warehouses and factories. It looked like an old industrial park; all of the buildings were made of brick and fire escapes ran up and down the sides. There were no signs indicating where this place was.

"It's just down here," Iona said, pointing down the curb.

"Wait," Orianna said "We'll want to blend in. Here." With a graceful wave of her hand, a shower of golden glitter flew out of her hand, toward Iona and me. I was caught flat-footed, but Iona scrambled, her vampire reflexes engaged to dodge the spray of sparkling particles.

Didn't matter. The glitter followed her, chasing her like a golden snowstorm, and covering her over in a sparkling sheen. As it settled over her, she spoke, with absolute venom of a kind that made me want to take a step back. "What did you *do?*"

"Just a little glamour to brighten you up," Orianna said with a smile. But she was hovering about ten feet off the ground, where, presumably, even Iona would have some difficulty getting to her.

Glamour indeed. The glitter had not been the mere human variety. It was a Faerie spell of illusion, and the illusion...was impressive.

Iona was still Iona, and she'd always been pretty, but what Orianna did made her look somehow way better. Her hair was shining, perfectly straight, hanging all the way to the middle of her back. When she moved, it flowed in perfect, straight sheets, and looked as soft as silk. Her amber eyes were bright and there was a fresh application of makeup where there hadn't been any before. She now wore a sleek dress that fell just above her knee, strapless and deep blue, and on her wrist perched the most expensive handbag I had ever seen.

I blinked, and the image wavered; Iona was back to being haggard, jacket barely hiding a black-bloody shirt. My stomach dropped; I'd seen this sort of reaction before.

"You just trying to make us blend in?" I asked, turning to Orianna. She'd changed, too. She was back on the ground like a normal human, but now she was wearing a rather revealing number. Her hair was long, and she was wearing quite a few bling-y rings that sparkled in the streetlamps. No slouch in the looks department under normal circumstances, now the Unseelie had a look that screamed "Super-model." But without the eating disorder.

I froze, trying to eye myself in the Beetle's window reflection. What did I look like?

"This is necessary," Orianna said. "We won't get in otherwise."

Iona popped her hip out and frowned. "I looked better before."

"Can I borrow that dress sometime?" I asked.

She looked down at herself. "Whatever, I can't see it. Let's get a move on, shall we?"

We walked down the sidewalk toward a brick building on the corner that had been painted gray. An old hardware store sign hung above the glass double doors at the front, but those had been painted over, hints of light escaping the edges.

Iona turned down the alley beside the building. There was a sway to her walk that definitely wasn't there before. Graceful as she was, I suspected there was no way that she'd be able to walk in heels like the ones Orianna had glamoured her to wear. They were like spikes.

A crowd formed a line behind a rusted metal door, blocked off by a red velvet rope. I looked it over with surprise. "The velvet ropes thing is real? I always thought it was something they made up for movies."

"It's real," Iona said. "Hm, the bouncers are human. That's interesting."

I reached into my pocket and pulled the little wooden box from inside.

Iona's eyes caught it immediately. "What's that?"

"Just something that Lockwood and I picked up a few weeks ago," I said, shaking it. There was a distinct rattle. "Even though things had been peaceful for a while, he still was paranoid for the first few weeks. Stocked me up on everything I might need for any given situation." I popped the lid open and pulled out a single, dark gray nail.

Iona squinted at it. "Is that...iron?" Orianna flinched.

I nodded. "Yep. Just in case."

Iona nodded her head. "Trust Lockwood to keep you well protected."

Orianna seemed to withdraw. "Please keep that a safe distance from me."

"Don't worry," I said, dropping it back in the little box. I closed it and slid it home in my pocket, giving it a pat. "I hope we won't need it at all, but my hopes and dreams aren't exactly coming true lately." With a nod at the door, I said, "Do you think we'll be able to get in? Or are we waiting in line?"

Iona just shook her head. "Give the Fae girl credit. We're waiting in no lines tonight." With that pronouncement, she turned and walked right up to the bouncers. "You. Let us in."

It's hard for me to overstate the reaction when she came strolling up to them. I was used to being an awkward teenager, uncomfortable in my body, catching the occasional stray look from an oddball guy. The reaction when their eyes moved from Iona to Orianna, and then to me...

...Well, if it hadn't been so funny, it might have left me completely mortified.

Double takes. Eyes nearly popping out of heads. One of the guys grunted, leaning forward like he'd been physically struck in the gut. Or maybe lower.

I cringed to watch them, and one of the bouncers waved those closest to the door. "Out of the way, VIP guests trying to get through."

VIP? I'd never been very important in my life.

"Good evening, ladies," said one of the other bouncers with a sly grin. "Welcome to Coldsnap."

His friend was trying to deal with the line; there were a couple women in leather jackets that let out a chorus of boos in our general direction. "I've been waiting for three hours!" one of them said.

"VIPs. Step back," said the bouncer.

"Yeah, right," said the girl. "You're just letting them in because they're hot."

I was pretty sure no one had ever used that word to describe *me* before. I didn't argue, though, when the bouncers opened the door and let us pass inside.

As soon as we stepped through, I shivered. The temperature had dropped significantly, and the chill in the air stole the breath right out of my lungs. It escaped me in a cloud of mist, the like of which I hadn't seen since we left New York in the dead of winter.

"Okay, maybe this spell has its uses," Iona said as the heavy door closed behind us, leaving us in this...this wintery wonderland.

Every inch of the walls, floor, and stairs was painted black. White arrows on the walls glowed bright blue, and when I looked down, the white on my T-shirt seemed to glow, too. "Blacklights? Isn't that cliché?"

"Done a lot of clubbing, have you?" Iona asked, starting up the stairs. The banisters were made to look like frosted ice, and the higher we climbed, the colder it got.

When we reached the landing, I realized why, exactly, it was absolutely freezing.

It was a palace of ice. The tables, chairs, walls, and even the lights were all made from carved ice. Every surface was draped with blankets and pillows. Icy pillars were spread throughout the room, glowing with brilliant blue light. A mellow, mystical twinkling music filled the air, as if it were laced with cold, born from the frozen depths of a glacier. The air smelled like fresh snow, crisp and moist.

There was a huge chunk of ice right near the top of the stairs that was sparkling with an almost mirror-like surface. Iona peered at herself in it, touching her face, running her fingers through her hair. She stared at herself with utter fascination, presumably since she hadn't seen herself in forever. "I don't know how I normally look, but...I'm guessing this is an improvement."

"You normally look like the angry goth that time forgot," I said, peering at my own glamour. "So, yes, it's better."

My hair was perfect, my face completely unblemished. That annoying scar that was left over from the big fight in New York was gone. It was still me, in there. I recognized my teal eyes, and the wavy auburn hair...but it was like I had been put through the ultimate Instaphoto filter. I was the very best version of myself that I could have ever imagined.

Also...I *was* hot.

Everything that I had ever disliked about myself was gone or smoothed over. My knobby knees, my turned-up nose, the acne scars near my temples...

After a moment of captivation, my stomach sank.

It was just a glamour. As great as I looked, this wasn't *really* who I was. "Hey, Orianna?" I said. "Could you maybe drop the glamour now that we're inside?"

"Why?" Orianna said, a frown creasing her perfect features. "Don't you like it?"

"A little too much, I think." I couldn't tear my gaze away from my reflection. "I may go full Narcissus if I look at myself like this much longer."

Orianna nodded and as I stared at myself, the glamour

faded. She started to turn to Iona, hand raised to do the same.

"No, no, it's fine," Iona said, backing away, but unable to keep from looking in the reflection. "I can deal with it."

Waiters were wandering through the room, bathed in the blue fluorescent lights. They all were shirtless, tall with rippling pectoral muscles and abs so pronounced that I would have been able to see them through three layers of clothing.

Big, muscly man-cake dudes. And I could tell just by looking that all of them were Unseelie.

"My, it *is* cold in here," Iona said, eyeing the closest waiter as he walked by with a tray filled with drinks. He had a crooked grin on his face, his white hair pulled back in a loose ponytail at the nape of his neck. But that wasn't what she was looking at.

I arched a brow at her.

Well, she wasn't wrong.

We walked past a few of them, and I realized they were all covered in super fine white iridescent glitter that was glowing in the blacklights.

This was not a dance club, like all the vampires seemed to prefer. It was more of a lounge, with little sitting areas spread throughout. Everyone had some kind of glowing drink in hand, and glass plates filled with hors d'oeuvres and desserts filled the tables.

My stomach rumbled. When was the last time I had eaten?

"It's cool here," Iona said.

"Wow, such a pun, Iona," I said.

She stopped, sparing me a dirty look. "I was going to say that it's cool here because they serve vampires."

She walked up to the bar, a solid block of ice with slowly

changing colors emanating from within, and leaned against it. "Type A, please."

The faerie behind the counter didn't even bat an eye. He turned to a small wine cooler behind him and pulled out a dark blue bottle. He lifted an equally dark blue glass from one of the side shelves, and filled it halfway before sliding it across the bar to her. His movements were fluid and graceful, distinctly not human.

She laid down a ten dollar bill, and lifted the glass up to her lips. I turned away before I had to watch her drink it.

"How do we find your contact?" I asked Orianna. Even with my jacket, I was still chilly. Should have gone with jeans instead of shorts.

"Well, I have a description of him," she said.

"Okay. Do you know his name?"

"Yes," Orianna said, scratching her chin. "If only I could remember it..."

"Well, when you think of it, we can finally do what we came to do," I said.

Iona turned and looked at me. "So what's next, winged one?"

Orianna didn't even react. She was frowning at the floor.

"V something..." she said. "Vix? No...Vin?"

"Are you looking for the boss?" The bartender spoke, taking a sudden interest in our conversation. The air shimmered behind him, and for a brief moment, I caught a glimpse of blue hair and silvery wings. Then the glamour fell back in place.

"Who's the boss?" Iona said. "V?"

"The owner of this place," he said. "But no one knows about him. How'd you find out he was here?"

Orianna swelled with pride, and opened her mouth to give her spiel about the Winter Court when I stopped her.

"We need some information," I said. "It's important."

The bartender shook his head, forbidding as a block of ice. "It's always important." He glanced around the room, checking to make sure that no one was paying attention. "Normally I would toss you out, but...a vampire, an Unseelie, and a human here together? I think the boss would find this just weird enough to want to see you."

"Oh, thank you," Orianna said.

The bartender's look was darkly amused. "You might thank me after you meet him. This way." And he beckoned us behind the bar, to follow him.

Orianna went after him immediately; if her wings had been out, I suspect they would have been fluttering happily.

Iona and I just exchanged glances, a sort of jaded look I was getting all too familiar with. The bartender's warning was...worrying, to say the least, especially for a girl who already had a full slate of problems. Why, I wondered, as I followed Orianna, did everything have to be so damned complicated?

16

"Vis! That's his name," Orianna exclaimed as the bartender led us behind the counter and through a frost covered swinging door. Mist permeated from vents at the floor, shrouding my worn shoes. The hall looked like something straight out of Faerie, clashing with the décor of the Winter Palace-slash-industrial nightclub.

There were stones below our feet as clear as crystal, but not slippery like ice. They shimmered with a rainbow hue, as if they were clear pearls. The walls shone like a mirror, but were tinged blue. Orbs of white light extended out of ice stalactites, and the ceiling over them was intertwined with wooden arches like some ancient Nordic meadhall.

The bartender turned and glared at Orianna. "It is not wise to speak his name so carelessly. The boss likes his privacy. Disrespect it, and you disrespect him."

"No disrespect intended," I said. Now that we were out of the blacklights, I realized that his skin didn't just appear blue; it was blue, like he had been doused in silver-cerulean paint.

The hall was lined with doors, or at least I thought it

was, because there were door-like shapes carved out of the perfectly smooth green walls every few feet. I wished Lockwood were here. He could have explained to me what all this was. He should have been paid as a Faerie tour guide for me. I made a note to ask Dad if we could give Lockwood a gift card or something to thank him for his work with me thus far. Hard to tell what he'd want, though; did he even use product in his hair, or was it all a glamour?

There was a door at the end of the hall, which I realized had slowly doubled in width and height as we had walked, all without me noticing. Now it appeared to be perfect white marble French doors with golden handles. The bartender pushed open the doors and stepped inside with an extremely deferential bow. "Boss...you have guests."

I stared past him into the room, the cold from the lounge still hanging in the air. Did ice faeries just exude cold? I was suddenly glad that we didn't have to meet with fire faeries, especially after my experience in a Summer jail. The room beyond was like the inside of an igloo. The walls were packed with snow, and little flakes fell from the ceiling, which was domed overhead.

There was a monstrous desk in the middle of the room, a solid slab of white like snow. Two muscly faeries stood on either side, but unlike the waiters out in the lounge, they were dressed in sharp black suits, like Nordic bodybuilders.

"Eh?" said a voice. It was deep, rasping, as if someone had smoked seven packs a day since they left the womb. "And who might that be?"

I was confused. I could hear the voice, but couldn't see who it belonged to.

I looked up, looked to either side...no sign of the speaker.

Iona elbowed me in the ribs and jutted her chin toward the desk. A chair was behind it, covered in thick furs, but no one was sitting in it. I squinted, and after a moment, real-ized...actually, someone *was* there.

A pixie, no bigger than my hand, hovered above the seat, his face just visible over the edge of the marble desk. He had a distorted, wide face with beady little eyes and a bald head. His wings were bright green, and made a soft sound like wind chimes as he fluttered them to stay aloft. He had a full-sized cigar clamped between his jaws, tendrils of smoke drifting up in front of his face.

I didn't know whether to groan or to laugh. I snorted instead, which I hastily turned into a cough. Iona clapped my back a little too hard, almost knocking me to my knees.

The boss, Vis, as Orianna had remembered, glowered at us from behind the desk. He was about the size of an action figure, or one of those hideous Bratz dolls.

"What do you want?" he asked, a sneer firmly in place. "And how did you find out about my sanctum sanctorum?"

I looked over at Orianna. She was the one who'd wanted to come here in the first place, right? Why wasn't she saying anything?

"Well?" the pixie asked. "Answer me." The guards on either side of him flexed their muscles.

"We came for your help," Iona said as I opened my mouth to speak.

"A vampire," said Vis. "Interesting. With a human and a fellow Unseelie, no less."

Orianna straightened her shoulders and thankfully, finally found her voice. "We need your help. Something has gone desperately wrong in Faerie, and–"

The pixie boss held up his tiny, pencil-sized arm and shook his head. "Nah. I don't wanna hear about it. There ain't no point. I left Faerie behind. What do I care what happens there now?" He turned his eyes on me. "And who is this human who seems entirely unimpressed by the fact that I am a pixie? Or by her surroundings, for that matter? Is she your thrall?" he asked, looking at Iona.

"Hey, I'm no one's slave," I said.

He leaned back on his arms, crossing his little legs as if he were sprawled out on a sun lounger. "I don't really care. You all are trespassing and have yet to give me a good reason to not throw you out."

"Yeah, well, I go where I am not wanted all the time," I said.

His sneer faltered for a second, then he sat up. Staring at me, he floated over the desk and across the room. Hovering in the air, eye level with me, he pulled the cigar out of his mouth with both hands. It was as big around as a tree trunk to him. He spewed smoke into the air. "Wait a second...you're the girl who's killing all the vampires, aren't you?"

It seemed that my reputation was starting to precede me. I folded my arms over my chest, hoping the nail in my pocket didn't make too much sound. "What of it?"

He shrugged, turning back toward his desk. "Nothing, really. Just find it interesting. Didn't think I'd get a chance to lay eyes on yah myself."

"Well, if you know anything about me, then you'll know that I usually am knee-deep in crazy stuff that goes on around Tampa," I said, dipping my hand in my pocket to find the little wooden box. "We were hoping we could have a few minutes of your time–"

"I really don't care," he said with a chuckle, popping the cigar back in his mouth. "And you're starting to test my patience. I don't like it when my patience is tested."

Well now he was just being rude.

He gestured to the guards on either side of him, and they started making their way toward us.

"I need you to listen to me for just a couple of minutes," I said, eyeing the Unseelie that was making his way toward me. His eyes were bright, full of violence. "If you don't...you're going to regret it."

"What are you going to do, *vampire slayer?*" The pixie boss threw back his little head and cackled. "Stake me?" With a wave of his hand he gestured to his guards. "Take care of them."

His guard reached out to grab me. I reached up and grabbed his arm with one hand, and with the other, drove the iron nail home right between the little bones on his wrist. There was a mangled cry of pain as the faerie poofed into a cloud of sparkling dust, which fell to the floor gently and silently like a soft rain. It covered the floor.

That was a surprise. I'd expected him to bleed, maybe to shout in pain, sizzle as the painful iron met his Fae skin. Instead, he'd burst like a glitter pinata, and I stepped back, because he was getting in my hair.

The guard that had latched onto Iona had stopped, staring down at the powdery glitter that had once been his colleague. Iona didn't look like she was struggling much. In fact, she looked more annoyed than anything. As usual.

Lockwood had told me about the effect of iron on faeries back when we had crossed the borders between our worlds. He said that it absorbed their magic, their essence. It was like an anti-magic.

He didn't say anything about turning fae to shiny dust, though.

I twirled the nail between my fingers like all the cool kids used to do with their pencils, while screaming in my heart because I'd just killed someone...or at least some*thing.* "Yeah," I said, "something like that." I resisted the temptation to blow on the nail as if it were a smoking revolver.

"Should have gone with *nailed it,*" Iona said. The guard was frozen beside her, as if afraid to take one more step.

"I thought about it, you know?" I said, still holding the nail in my sweating palm. Had I really just killed another Fae? I mean, one that clearly had no problem with violence, but still? "It's so '80's action movie, though. Felt a little too on the nose."

Iona nodded. "We live in subtler times, it's true."

Vis was gaping at us. His cigar had tumbled out of his mouth and bounced across the desk, smearing ash on the pristine marble.

I looked over at Orianna, who appeared just as shocked as Vis. "Go ahead," I said. "We've got his attention now."

Orianna glanced down at the pile of glitter on the floor and swallowed nervously.

"Oh, and if we don't like your answers," I looked back at Vis, "it is going to look like a glitter bomb went off in here when I get done."

Vis shifted uncomfortably, his wings fluttering even more furiously in the air. His glare was back in place, and his brow knit together in one angry line.

"We really don't mean you any harm," Orianna said, clearly not down with my approach of bringing shock and violence and turning Vis's henchmen into glitter bombs. "We just want to know what's been going on with Summer."

Vis's eyes flashed with recognition. "What do I know about summer? Well, it's warm. Lasts about...all year around here? Eleven months, maybe?"

I glared at him, flashing the nail again. "What did I say about not liking your answers? Oh, that's right. You'll be confetti for some kid's birthday party by tomorrow."

"Okay, okay," he said, and fluttered down to pick up his cigar, giving it a good dusting off before he put it back in his little mouth. His eyes narrowed, but his tone was steady. "All I've heard are rumors. Why do you care, though? It isn't as if court politics affects you."

I shrugged. "I've been asked to help."

"And you just come running anytime someone asks, huh? Who asked you?" He nodded at Orianna. "Her?"

"No," I said. "The Queen of the Winter Court. Now why don't you tell us what you know?"

His eyes widened. Didn't see that one coming, did he? He drew in another breath from the cigar, which was still lit. He puffed out the smoke, and then sighed. "There's been turmoil in the Seelie part of Faerie ever since they had that incident a while back. Nothing you need to worry yourself about, just internal business."

"You mean when they tried that Paladin, Lockwood?" I asked.

He almost dropped the cigar again. "You...are shockingly well-informed. For a human," he added. "Fine. Seems you know. But did you know this? Something happened in that room to completely destroy the authority of Summer."

I felt Iona's gaze on the side of my face, and it took all of my strength to not look back at her. Yeah, yeah, I got it. That was me.

"The Seelie Queen was disgraced in front of all of her nobles and the Winter Court," Vis said. "This is not politics as usual. This was not tea and crumpets. This was an atom bomb going off under your frigging seat."

"Who is Adam Bomm?" Orianna asked, looking very earnestly at him.

Vis chuckled. "I can see this one's fresh over the barrier. Anyway, I haven't kept up with the most recent news. We don't get a lot of visitors from Faerie. Although..." His little face turned pensive.

"Although what?" I said.

"I must admit, I have seen more fae moving to this world, fleeing whatever is happening there." He shrugged. "Summer Fae, too, unlike myself. Of course, Florida's perfect for them. Very insular community, though. Like those Amish werewolves. Or those tribes in the Amazon. Maybe a little more cross-cultural connection here, though.

"Yes, that's the trouble," Orianna said with a frown. "No one seems to know what exactly it is that is happening."

Vis hesitated, tapping the cigar. A pile of ash dropped on the already-dirty marble. "I might have heard...one little rumor that could explain things." He sucked a big breath of smoke in, and squeaked, "Maybe."

My heart skipped a beat. "Well," I said, "spill it."

"It's just a rumor," Vis said, taking his sweet time, seeming to enjoy keeping me in suspense, "but the word was that after all that humiliation for the Seelie..." and his eyes seemed to glow in pleasure like the end of his cigar, "...that the Summer Queen has been deposed."

17

W e left Vis smoking in his office without turning any more Winter Fae into glittersparkles. The cold had settled on my bones, the chill really nipping at my bare legs. I didn't think I'd ever been so happy to step back out into the sweltering Florida heat. Iona gave one last longing glance over at the bar as we passed. "What, you need more O-Neg?" I asked.

"I don't often get to order anything out," she said. "It's more about the experience for me."

"Wow, Cassie, I mean, *wow,*" Orianna said as we made our way down the stairs. "You were just...wow."

"I didn't do anything that amazing," I said, even as I was flattered.

"The way you wielded that iron...you were fearless," Orianna said. "It's – it's away in that little box again, right? Please keep it away from me."

"It's away, yes," I said. "Just don't make me angry." She paled a little. "Kidding."

A confused look past over her face. "But you're dressed like an adult."

"'Kidding' means making a joke," I said. "I'm not serious. I'm trying to be funny."

She looked disgruntled. "Killing me is funny to you?"

"I think it was," Iona said as we stepped out into the sticky heat of the Tampa night. The bouncers barely spared us a glance as we made our way out of the alley toward the car. "You did okay in there," Iona said. I didn't know if she knew, but Orianna had dissolved her glamour. She kept tossing her hair over her shoulder. It was still a sight, but I think she thought she was even more dazzling still. "That whole conversation seemed to be trending toward entropy, but you really turned it around with some random violence." She nodded. "I approve."

"Thanks, I guess," I said. "Kinda wish it hadn't gone that way. Is it wrong that I feel guilty for glitter-dusting that guy?"

"No," Orianna said.

"Yes," Iona said. "You could tell by looking at him that he'd not only done his fair share of harm in his life, he was about to happily do some more to us."

I shook my head. "I don't know what it is, but every time I run into anyone new anymore, they all seem to know who I am. And half of them want to kill me."

"Yeah, you don't take out the vampire Lord of the territory and go unnoticed," Iona said.

"But why did he assume that it was me?" I said.

"How many other humans do you see hanging out with faeries and vampires on a regular basis?" Iona asked. "Or ever? We're not exactly a multicultural bunch."

"Point," I said. "I guess I didn't realize that faeries would be interested in vampire affairs at all."

"Normally, vampires and faeries don't get along all that well I hear," Orianna said. "But I can imagine that there are situations where they need to come together sometimes, trade information and things like that."

"Information is worth more than money to people like us," Iona continued. "Which is why Vis was so resistant to giving us any. We didn't really give him much in return, thankfully."

"Well, aside from a disintegrated guard," I said. "Sorry you had to see that, Orianna." My mind flashed back to the night I saw Mill in full beast mode killing that human on the sidewalk outside of the restaurant. My stomach clenched and the knots around my heart tightened like a noose. "I know how difficult that kind of thing can be."

Orianna shrugged as we kept moving down the sidewalk toward the Beetle. "It's not the first time I've seen a death. But it is the first time I've seen the potency of iron used here on Earth."

Another memory clouded my vision: that of Calvor, the Fae whose face I'd dissolved with a great gob of bloody, iron-bearing spit when he'd tried to kill me. I shuddered; it was not a happy memory.

"Well, all I have to say is that you really should be careful about putting pressure on people like Vis," Iona said.

"Why?" I said. "I thought you said I handled myself pretty well in there."

Iona came to a full and abrupt stop. "That's why."

I followed her eye.

"Oh, come on," I said, groaning.

A whole line of ex-pat Unseelie – shirtless, buff, and blue – were standing in front of Iona's car, waiting for us.

18

"I knew it was too good to be true," I said, standing on a chilly Tampa street with a line of blue-skinned, shirtless Winter Fae boys standing menacingly between us and Iona's VW Beetle. "Guess you were right, Iona. Information does come at a cost."

"Get them!" came a shriek over our heads, echoing down the empty street.

I looked up and saw Vis flitting around above our heads. He was doing figure eights and pointing at us by the light of a flickering streetlamp.

The minions loitering near the car started toward us. Some were loosely carrying baseball bats, others had brilliantly colored lights in their hands. Magic, I assumed. Because of course they had to make it complicated. I sighed. Could I not have one encounter with someone in power without it ending in a royal rumble? I fished the iron nail from my pocket, holding it out in front of me like the world's tiniest dagger.

"She's got iron!" Vis shrieked, his voice comically distorted as it bounced off the brick and metal of this industrial district. He sounded tinny and borderline-hysterical, and shook his tiny fists at us, careful to stay far out of our reach. His warning made the goons a little more wary, and they slowed their progress toward us, like sharks slowly moving through the water toward prey.

"Oh, let's get this over with," Iona said, and darted toward a pair of them closest to her. She slammed into them like a linebacker, and they were bowled over into the gutter. Taking Iona's signal, Orianna darted toward another cluster of them at high speed, wings fluttering. They responded by sending magic bolts at her, light flashing off the nearby brick facades.

The last four – those with the baseball bats – came for me.

Of course they'd come after me, the fragile human. If one of those bats hit me upside the head, it was going to be lights out Cassie. And then I'd end up – well, I didn't know how I'd end up. Probably minced and served in the appe- tizers at Coldsnap. Or maybe I'd just be the source of the vampire refreshments for a night or two, assuming they didn't accidentally bleed me out all over the street.

I held my nail in front of me like sword and shield. Would the iron absorb their magic before it even hit me? It didn't seem to matter, because they weren't throwing it, they were leading with the bats. This made no sense to me, because if I'd had magic, I'd have been zapping and blasting everywhere I went. Product of being stuck in a few too many situations where I felt helpless and hopeless with nothing but my hands and wits, I suppose.

The first Fae took a long windup and swung at me from a distance that might as well have been at Tropicana Field. To say he missed me by a mile was understating it; Orlando was closer than his swing. That said – it was a strong one. If my head had been in the path, it'd have landed somewhere around Toledo. Which might have been worse than the hit, honestly.

Still, good. I was going to be able to avoid the hits if I saw them coming. As long as only one of them swung at a time, I'd be able to duck as they powerswung their way into the Unseelie baseball Hall of Fame.

Hopefully.

I wondered how Lockwood would feel if I asked him for a nail gun. And if my dad would be willing to buy me one. He wasn't very handy, so it's not like he'd have one to give me. But I really could have used one.

Another of the faeries swung, closer this time, and I leapt out of the way. The bat collided with a lamppost beside me, and the dent that it left sent a chill down my spine. It bent the top of the pole at a thirty-degree angle. That could have been me. My arm. My leg. I could have been on my way to Toledo, a fate worse than hell.

I tried to poke the nail at them, but they were a lot faster than me, jumping away, flapping their wings to stay aloft. They hissed like angry cats, and swung at a distance, clearly afraid I'd turn them to sparkly powder. Which I was absolutely going to do if they got close enough and I avoided being Home Run'd to the worst part of Ohio (kind of an oxymoron, I know; are there any good parts of Ohio?)

Vis was flying over our heads, screaming his little lungs out. "Come on, there's only three of them! What's taking you so long?"

"Unfair that you guys have a cheering section," I said, jumping up the curb as another one tried to Grand Slam me. "I should have home field advantage."

Out of the corner of my eye, I could see Iona was holding her own against the three she was fighting. She was blocking their strikes, taking baseball bat hits to the arms, the legs, the thudding of metal against flesh sickening in the night. She seemed to be unable to land any blows of her own, but her grunts were more perfunctory and less pained.

Orianna's battle had gone to the sky, and above us I could see flashes of magic being traded over the street. The snap of a spell hitting a brick facade was followed by a small *pop!* that resulted in a couple bricks falling onto the street. They were blasting at each other, but seemed to be controlling their fire, trying to strike for maximum impact, not firing all willy-nilly. I wondered if they had an ammo limit, like a gun.

Still, Vis was right. There were only three of us. There were a dozen of them. And they had magic.

I ducked again as one of the faeries – this one the biggest of them all, his chest seemingly as wide as Iona's VW – swung his bat at me, and the bat just skimmed my hair. "Hey, I'm not looking for a new stylist." I jumped up straight again, and desperate for some leg up in the fight, lobbed the nail at the faerie in front of me.

It bounced off his bare chest, and his flesh seared where it struck. He cried out, dropping his bat, and ducked backward, clutching at the nail-shaped burn sizzled on his chest. The other three faeries spared him only a glance before they charged at me again.

Well, three faeries were better than four. The nail-burnt one had fallen to his knees under a street light, sparkling glitter flowing off his chest like somewhere Thanos had snapped for the Fae.

I was panting, jumping backward, trying to keep out of the way, when I bumped into a wall. My bare leg grazed brick and mortar.

Crap. Cornered.

"I need that nail," Iona shouted, buried in a scrum with three Fae.

"I threw it," I called back, bracing myself. The three Fae with bats were grinning, and setting themselves up in a semi-circle, surrounding me in place against the wall.

Iona tossed me a murderous sort of look. "Great." Flashes overhead told me Orianna was still tangoing with her quarries.

No help was coming.

Vis was shrieking with delight overhead. "Finish them off! Finish them off!" I wondered if he'd have a cigar afterward to celebrate.

Two of the Faeries took a swing at me at once, and I fell to the ground, holding my hands over my head. The bats plowed into the brick, send a shower of chips over me like frigging faerie dust. I was on my side, nowhere to hide, nowhere to run, and I could feel them looming over me.

Welp, it'd been a good run, I suppose. Kinda sad to have bested vampires and werewolves only to be brought down by a bunch of guys who looked like they spent more time on their abs and hair than they did reading books, but I suppose maybe that was the natural fate of any teenage girl who got a little too out of control. Just...maybe not quite in the way that I was coming to my end. This was decidedly less fun, I suspected. There were no motorcycles, recreational drug use, or teenage pregnancies. Just a baseball bat to the head for me, and then lights out–

A golden light flashed everywhere. For a split second, I thought the final blow had been struck, and my skull had exploded open like the Walmart doors at five am on Black Friday. I blinked against the sudden brightness, holding my hands up to shield my eyes.

The faeries with bats turned their heads to look for the

source of this light. I saw one of them struck in the chest by a blast of magic and he was thrown back as if a car had struck him. Another took a hit; he went flying sideways into the wall, bat clattering to the sidewalk beside my head.

"Surcease, you blackguards!" rang a heavenly voice over the street. It was like a choir of angels, if they could all be distilled into one voice. A glowing figure appeared overhead, wings stretching out from a well-muscled chest, a bright golden aura coming off this radiant figure. He fired another blast of golden light and the last of the bat-bearing Fae crumpled in front of me. "How dare you so mistreat our champion! You will come to rue your villainous conduct of this day, I assure you."

The man was pointing at Vis, who had stopped screeching, and was staring at the newcomer in shock.

His glow seemed to fade as he descended on those fluttering, angelic wings. Now I could see his face – lantern jaw, perfect, dimpled chin. Long, golden hair fluttered behind him as if pushed by a fan. He held out his palm, and a ball of blue light appeared on it.

"Who are you?" Vis asked, mouth open like he was waiting for a cigar to just fly in.

The new faerie didn't even answer. He just tossed the blue light at Vis. Vis dodged, and the spell smashed into the sign for the old hardware store, causing it to explode. Vis didn't wait around to see this happen; he took off through the night, leaving only a trail of obscenities behind him.

This new, golden faerie, sunbeams seeming to come from him like a halo, landed lightly on his feet before me. A chorus might have sung. Or my head might have been ringing.

Where Mill had been dark and brooding and secretive, this faerie was warm and smiling and bright. His eyes were so blue they put Xandra's to shame. Almost glowing, when I stared into his, I felt a shock of something quiver through me, from tingles on my scalp all the way down to my toes, stopping at all points between.

He held out his hand to me, his bright eyes wide with concern. "Are you all right, my lady?"

19

I had always loved the princess stories as a little girl. You know the ones; filled with dragons and castles and magic. For a solid year between six and seven, I asked my dad to read the same story over and over to me every single night. "Daddy?" I asked on one of those nights, summery and sweet, like those Upstate New York eves tended to be. "Are knights real?"

He smiled at me, and patted my blankets affectionately. "I suppose. There are people who are kind, brave, strong and generous, and go out of their way to help others. More than anything, they're selfless. They're rare, but they do exist."

"Maybe I'll meet a knight one day," I said, pretty well satisfied that not only would I meet one someday, but maybe I'd marry one, too. If I didn't get my hands on the king, first.

For some reason, that memory was as clear as if it had happened yesterday when I took the golden faerie's hand and allowed him to help me to my feet. He was smiling, eyes fixed on me as if I were the only person in the entire world.

"Yeah, I'm – " why was my brain having a hard time forming the word? "I'm fine, yes. How are you?" My face scrunched up – had I really just asked him that? I sounded like an airhead.

He smiled with relief. "I am well, and very glad to hear this. I would have been devastated had you been injured in any way. That dastardly pixie will much rue the day he made effort to harm you." He snapped to attention. "But you must forgive me, I have forgotten my manners." A step back, and he bowed low, sweeping wide with one arm out. "Lady Cassandra, my name is Aureus. I am the White Knight of Summer."

"Summer?" I said. No wonder Vis took off. And that title. If I had never been to Faerie, I might have been properly impressed at his archaic lingo and grandiose gestures. "Well, your timing was...really great." I sounded so lame. Stupid.

There was an annoyed click beside me. I glanced over at Orianna glaring at Aureus.

"But of course, milady," he said with a wide grin. "I am glad that I made it here in time. I would never have forgiven myself if anything had happened to you. Do not fear." He rattled a sword hanging from his belt. "I shall protect you hence, even unto death."

"What about after death?" Iona asked, edging into my view. She had lots of black speckled over her clothing from the melee with the Unseelie. "How do you feel about protecting a girl after she dies?"

Aureus cocked his head. "I'm sorry, I'm afraid I don't understand."

"It's better that way," I said. "What brings you here, exactly? And with such magnificent timing."

"Ah, yes," he said, then seemed to become captivated by something behind me. Or on my nose, maybe. "You are even more beautiful than you were described," he said, almost breathless. "Your hair is like the softest silk, shimmering in the light. And your eyes are like the heartiest of summer leaves, brilliantly green as the sunlight shines upon them."

I couldn't help it. I blushed. Who had described me as beautiful in Faerie? I thought they all hated me there. And compared to pretty much every faerie I have ever seen ever, I was like a muddy hog surrounded by thoroughbred horses.

This drop dead gorgeous White Knight guy...he thought I was pretty? I flushed even more. "How...how did you find me?" I said, running my hands through my hair and finding it not-so-silky. I managed to flush out a few pebbles, actually, and some sand.

"I was told to look for a great battle, my Lady. You would likely be at the center of it, as you were during your time in Faerie."

"Oh." I hesitated, and then closed my mouth. "Well. You got me there."

I looked down at him and saw his wardrobe for the first time. His face had completely taken me off guard, so much so that I hadn't noticed the white sheet wrapped across his chest, toga-style, and bound with a golden rope. Straight out of a frat party. A sexy, sexy frat party. "Oh, my," I said. "This outfit is not going to do."

His smile faltered. "Does my appearance not please you?"

I looked down at one exposed pectoral muscle. "Well, it works for me, but, uh...larger society...you aren't going to blend in very well." I looked down at his feet, perfect toes peeking through the Egyptian-style sandals. "The sandals work."

He looked down at himself. "My deepest apologies, Lady

Cassandra. I did not mean to present myself in an unbe-coming manner."

"There is absolutely nothing wrong with what you are wearing," Iona said, so-very-firmly. "But if you need help changing to something a bit more of-our-world, I am happy to assist you with my own expertise. In fact, I would be willing to go so far as to step into the changing room with you and a dozen or so potential outfits, really offer you quality feedback, go through some mixing and matching–"

I blinked at her. "Um...what?"

"It's called being friendly," Iona said, interposing herself between me and him. She turned to Aureus and flashed him a beautiful smile. It lit up her whole face, and her amber eyes were bright in the light emanating off of him. Wow. She really was pretty when she wasn't scowling. "Hi. I'm Iona. Lady Cassandra's friend and basically the only reason that she's still alive."

"Wow," I said softly, under my breath.

Aureus took her hand in both of his and brought it to his lips, kissing the back of it delicately. "Well met. And thank you for keeping this marvelous lady safe until I could arrive."

"You are very welcome," Iona said – and giggled.

Iona *giggled*.

He turned his attention back to me, and when his eyes met mine, again there was a chill that ran down my spine. Even when I was with Mill, he rarely looked at me like that. I really didn't know how to handle it. My head throbbed, and my vision went fuzzy for a second. I looked at Orianna, who was standing to my side, arms folded and quiet, pensive, watching Aureus, and suddenly I could see her with her glamour stripped away – her gold hair and eyes, her slitted pupils, her features just slightly off from those of a human.

In contrast, when I looked at Aureus, the White Knight was...exactly the same. Just as gorgeous as I'd first seen him. That was actually what he looked like.

I smiled at him, but scratched at my cheek.

"So...what is it with all of these faeries coming after me...tonight of all nights?"

He gave me a curious look. "You have had more than one visitor from my world this night?"

I nodded over my shoulder toward Orianna, who rolled her eyes and looked away as he turned to her.

"Ah, an Unseelie," he said, with a little more reservation. "I see that this matter happening in Faerie has involved both sides. And wearing a glamour, I see."

"Some of us try to blend in." Orianna's eyes narrowed, all of her usual pep turned icy. Her golden eyes were watching him like a dog watched a stranger walking up to their door.

"She's just testy because you caught us in the middle of trying to find the same sort of answers," I said.

Aureus's lips turned just slightly, producing the most subtle and beautiful frown. "Did the angry pixie know nothing as well?" He gestured toward Coldsnap.

"He told us the Summer Queen might have been deposed," I said. "That was the extent of his info."

His eyebrows rose. "Ill news indeed, if true. There was strife, but when I left she was still on the throne."

"When did you leave?" I asked.

"I was dispatched some time ago," Aureus said. "I am unclear how long. I was told your time is very different than ours. Also, I spent some amount of days in front of something you call a 'telee-visor.' I saw many wondrous things on this mystical portal, stories out of a land called Nit-Flix, where both the mundane and the bizarre seem to coexist shoulder to shoulder."

I blinked at him a few times, but it might maybe have looked like I fluttered my eyelids. "You watched Netflix? For how long? And with who?"

"A lovely older lady named Gladys who called me her Hun-E," Aureus said. "I believe that's a sort of mystical defender. The ceremonial role included keeping her warm during 'Nit-Flix binges.' She allowed me the use of a lovely guest chambers in her castle, fed me the most delicious meals prepared by an expert chef called Ubur Etes, whose food was the most delectable I've ever tasted, and we sat upon her couch indulging for...well, it was perhaps longer than it should have been. I may have been entranced." He frowned. "I think perhaps she was a witch of some stripe, and skilled at that. Still, I bear her no ill will, even for the clothes of mine that she lost, repeatedly, while laundering them."

Iona's face twitched. "Did she make you sit around naked while she did – I mean lost – your laundry?"

"Yes," Aureus said, nodding furiously. "It was the oddest thing. I asked if she needed to take them to the river to see it done properly, and she did – but she swore her grip was weak, and the current took them away. I believed her, because when she laid her hand upon me, indeed, there was some weakness in her grasp as she showed me by putting it upon my thigh and squeezing. Truly, I do fear for her, and suggested she see a healer, immediately."

"I'm guessing she was already feeling much better after that," Iona said.

I rubbed my temple. "Uhm. Okay. There's a lot to unpack here, but first I'm gonna say...Aureus, much as you

just helped me, maybe you should head back to Faerie."
Iona shot me an absolutely scandalized look. "I'm not sure
you're ready for Earth."

"I cannot," Aureus said, smiling. "I would be doing a
great dishonor to my people if I were to return before I
accomplished my quest. I'm afraid I must assist you and see
this task done, else I would be forced into exile."

"With Gladys?" I asked.

"I suppose, since I would have nowhere else to go,"
Aureus said. "She did warn me that the next time I returned
I would need to make a trip with her to a place called 'Fun-
key town.' I am uncertain where that is. Perhaps somewhere
north of here. Regardless, I have a quest to complete, and
thus no time for 'Fun-key town' while Faerie hangs in the
balance."

"Mmmmmm," Iona said, sounding very much like a car
purring. "Funkytown. Well played, Gladys."

I tried to keep the straightest face I could. "So, what was
going on in Faerie when you left? Why did they send you?"

"The events of the Summer Court have indeed left it in
turmoil, but this crisis expands by the terrible things
bleeding over from Earth," Aureus said.

"What is bleeding over?" I asked.

"Terrible things," he said with a shudder. "Human artifacts are showing up in our woods, in our fields, in our
domiciles. Last week, a Summer child came wandering into
the castle carrying this." And with a flourish, he pulled a cell
phone out of...somewhere. Hell if I knew where. "At first it
would light up and howl madly at the strangest intervals.
We thought it demon-made, demon-possessed, but the
Court Viziers correctly identified it as a human artifact
known as a Sil-Fune." He showed me the cracked display. "I
slayed it in personal combat, naturally, silencing it forever."

"Usually I just press the button on the side for that," Iona said, "but I've often felt a desire to do the same."

Aureus went on, undeterred. "The court is worried that the wards will fail enough for humans themselves to find their way into faerie, bringing their iron with them to destroy us." I could see the tension in his eyes as he looked pleadingly at me. "Naturally, they sent their greatest warrior to see this threat ended – and here I am."

"And they sent you to talk to me?" I asked, giving Orianna a look out of the corner of my eye. She was kicking at the ground, not daring look at me. "Why?"

"Although there have been expatriates who have left Summer and come to your world," Aureus said, "none return with enough knowledge to safely steer us in this kingdom of yours. The few who do maintain contact are affiliated with other kingdoms – that of Acapulco, for instance. Very popular with Summer exiles." He looked me in the eye. "You are the only person in this place that we know, truly."

"Well, how do you know that Florida is the source of your problems?" I asked. "How do you know this cell phone showing up in your kingdom isn't straight out of, I dunno, Cancun or something." It was a big world, after all.

"Our seers tell our queen that our troubles come from here, in Tam-Pah," Aureus said with the shake of his head. "And who better to guide my hand to the foe I seek than the Iron Bearer of legend?"

"The problem is," I said, looking once more at Orianna, who was studiously avoiding my own gaze, "I don't know the foe you seek. I don't even know where to start with your issue. And I've got my own problems." I thought of Xandra, somewhere out there – alone, hopefully.

"If only you knew a Summer expat you could ask about all this," Iona said, oh-so-dryly.

I sighed. I'd tried to give Lockwood a break, really I had. But if the small army of Unseelie trying to beat my brains out with baseball bats hadn't convinced me that stumbling blind into the affairs of the Fae was a bad idea, the sudden appearance of this knight in shining...well, everything, did the trick. "Fine. We'll talk to Lockwood."

Suddenly, Aureus dropped to his knee. "Brave Lady Cassandra, perhaps in this we can give aid to each other in our mutual good cause."

Iona nudged me. "Please say yes, please say yes."

I looked over at her. What the hell, Iona?

She shrugged. "It would be cruel to send him back to Gladys. I respect her hustle and all, but he's so innocent."

"Fine," I said, and watched Orianna's shoulders slump. "You may join us, Sir Knight." Aureus seemed to glow at that. "Now let's go talk to someone who might actually know what's going on."

20

"Who is this Lockwood we are going to speak with?" Aureus asked. We'd ridden mostly in silence, a few astonished breaths here and there from Aureus and Orianna, their muttered exclamations about driving in a "horseless carriage" occupying their full attention and leaving Iona and me to exchange looks in lieu of our own mutterings.

Lockwood's house wasn't too far out of town, a small clapboard two story in a quiet neighborhood with a perfectly manicured yard. The wind had picked up, a chill in the air as I strode up the walk with a vampire and two faeries behind me.

It was hard to understate how weird my life had gotten these last few months. "Like stone, but with such perfect cuts," Aureus muttered, studying the concrete beneath our feet as we walked up the path. I rapped my knuckle on the door, then stood back and waited.

I ended up trying three more times before the door was yanked open, and a surly looking Lockwood peered out.

"What?" he snapped. But his gaze softened when he saw that it was me. "Oh. Cassandra."

"It's Lady Cassandra, you ungrateful–" I held up my hand to Aureus, stopping him in mid-sentence.

Poor angry, sleepy Lockwood. Crabby, sleepy Lockwood. It took him a few seconds of looking between my three taga-longs before he managed to come to any sort of conclusion about what he was seeing on his doorstep. "Come in, I suppose. I'll put the kettle on."

I stopped just over the threshold, my breath completely taken away. The last time I'd been here, it was like a forest, with trees and flowers and logs for furniture. Now it was like the inside of a castle, with sandstone walls, polished wooden floors, and draperies with golden stitching hanging from the high walls. Tall, thin windows overlooked what appeared to be a snowy mountainside.

Faeries and magic. Would I ever really get used to it?

He led us through to an enormous library that stretched above our heads for several stories, packed to the brim with books. Luxurious, overstuffed couches were clustered around a fireplace along with some high-backed chairs and polished wooden tables.

"So," Lockwood called from the next room while bidding us wait, "last I saw you but a few hours ago, you had one faerie companion. I see that you have somehow picked up another."

"Do you know him?" Iona asked.

"Just in passing," Lockwood said, reappearing through the open archway. A lavish kitchen waited just beyond, filled with modern human conveniences. Lockwood rubbed his eyes. "I can't get one bloody night of sleep..." he muttered under his breath. "This is my fate, I'm just cursed, I suppose."

"Lockwood?" I said.

"Yes?" he said in a far more pleasant tone than his grumbling. It was as if he didn't realize he was doing it.

"You don't by any chance have any more of those little pastries you had at my house, do you?"

"Of course," he said, peering out through the door at us, a smile on his face. "I'll bring them out in just a moment when I get the stove on."

I sunk down into one of the chair and sighed with happiness. It was probably the most comfortable chair I had ever sat in in my life. I could have fallen asleep sitting up. I hadn't realized just how exhausted I was.

"So," Lockwood said as he reappeared; at first I thought by magic, then I realized I'd dozed off, and I didn't even know for how long. Tea cups steamed on the table in front of me, and delicious pastries waited beside them. "How did this...unfortunate grouping come to be?" He offered a look of pure disdain to Orianna, and something...else...for Aureus.

I told him about the manic pixie mob boss at Coldsnap, about rumors regarding the Queen of Summer, and how they'd attacked us on our way out. I also added the bit about Aureus coming to our rescue, and Lockwood's eye twitched in the telling for some reason. It might have had something to do with Iona idly fingering her neck while she listened. If she could have been panting, she would have been, I suspected.

"How is it," Lockwood asked, pinching the bridge of his nose, "that you manage to upset every person that you meet, Cassandra?"

"I don't upset *everyone*," I said. "I didn't upset the Oracle."

"For which we are very fortunate," Lockwood said. He

had dark circles under his eyes, no glamour applied.

My heart sank as I looked at him. "I'm sorry we woke you up."

He waved a hand dismissively. "I told you to call me if you needed me. *Call*, specifically. But this, I suppose, is almost the same." He offered a pained look as he glanced around. "I could have tidied up, though."

I looked around the beautiful library, with the crackling fire roaring in the hearth. There was literally nothing out of place. My mother couldn't have found fault with his house-keeping. "Oh, yeah," I said, "it's a total wreck. You should be ashamed of yourself."

"So, this is where the famous exiled Paladin has made his home," Aureus said with a broad smile. "You have not lost your magical touch since leaving Faerie, I see."

"I take it that you are here for the same reason as Orianna, correct?" Lockwood asked Aureus.

"Indeed," he said. "I am searching for the origin of the trouble on Earth."

"How can you be certain that the origin is here, and not in Faerie?" Lockwood asked.

"That was the original theory," Aureus said. "But when the boundaries began to blur and human artifacts began to make their way into our world, the court realized that the trouble must have been coming from here."

Lockwood shook his head. "This doesn't make any sense. And what of the Court? Has the Autumn Queen assumed the throne?"

Aureus's face fell. "When I left, the Summer Queen still sat upon the throne. Though according to Lady Cassandra – or at least that pixie piece of offal who threatened her life – our noble Queen has been overthrown."

"Truly?" Lockwood looked at me with smoky eyes. "And you learned this from Vis?"

I nodded.

Lockwood frowned. "That place is a watering hole for ex-pats. Not just Winter Fae, either. He may indeed know what he's talking about."

"I didn't see a water hole," Orianna said, still nibbling. "Everything was frozen, though."

"So what next?" I said, ignoring her. "We don't really know anything for certain, aside from the fact that Summer is in chaos and whatever is going on is causing our worlds to bleed together, blurring the lines."

"Yes. This is a rather unfortunate predicament, isn't it?" Lockwood scratched at his chin. "Cassandra, I am uncertain how to best address this situation. And I must ask – is this really the best use of your time and talents?"

I felt strangely stung by that; there were, of course, things I'd have preferred to be doing. Chasing Xandra, for one. Sleeping for another. Still, a gut-level truth welled up in me and I gave it voice: "Lockwood...can you say for certain that whatever trouble is coming out of Summer right now has nothing to do with what happened on our visit?"

Lockwood shifted in his seat, pained. "Those issues were bubbling far before we arrived, I can assure you of that. Whatever is occurring now may have little to do with our actions."

"Oh?" I said. "Then why do I keep hearing that we left everything in chaos?"

Lockwood looked over at Orianna for clarification.

"She's right," Orianna said. "Things have been tense, to say the least, since you left."

Lockwood thoughtfully rubbed his chin.

"The Summer Knight here tells me that I am as good as a hero there," I said. "How can this be unrelated?"

"Perhaps it is," he conceded.

"I need to be going," Iona blurted out. When I looked at her, she added, "It is going to be daylight soon, and I don't want to get stuck here all day."

I pulled my phone out of my pocket and checked the time. She was right. It was almost sunrise.

She rose to her feet, dusting off the front of her jeans. "I'll just leave you here with Lockwood. Is that all right?"

"Certainly," Lockwood said, but I could see that his smile was a little cooler than usual.

I rose, too, and walked with her to the door. "Thanks for all your help."

"I didn't really help much," Iona said, fingering the dried black blotches on her blouse. "I lost Xandra, didn't I?"

"I don't think you had any control over that," I said. "From what you said, she was completely out of her mind." It was hard to even say that out loud.

"She'll find a place to lay low for the day," Iona said. "Even if she just woke up, her vampire instincts are going to kick in. She won't like sunlight; she'll avoid it at all costs."

"I hope you're right," I said.

Iona grabbed the door handle. "We'll go hunting again tonight, pick up her trail. I'm sure by then you'll have shaken your way through all this Faerie nonsense." She looked over my shoulder toward the library, then leaned close, and in a hushed voice added, "Though if you happen to drag it out a bit, keep that shiny, shiny man around...I'd understand. And appreciate–"

"Ionaaaaaa." I added several syllables to her name, the fatigue getting to me. "I really don't want to deal with this Faerie business right now. I just want to go to bed."

"Speaking of," she said, "that Aureus is going to need a place to sleep."

"Ionaaaaaaaaa!"

"What? You can't send the poor man back to Gladys, she'll eat him alive!"

I just shook my head at her as she opened the door with a soft click. I turned to head back to the library but stopped because she'd just frozen there. Looking back, she was anchored to the threshold. "I thought you were leaving," I said. "Sunrise is in less than ten minutes."

"Yeah...I don't think so," she said, and beckoned me over.

I stood beside her, peering out into the suburban street. The entire sky overhead was completely covered in clouds, and it was pitch black. There was no hint of light on the horizon. A deepening chill swept through the summer air, making me cover my bare arms with my hands. "What is going on?" I asked, my whole body shuddering at the terrible, blustery, unseasonable cold.

21

"Well, this certainly can't be good," Lockwood said.

We were all standing out on the front lawn, a hideous wind cutting through hard, the mercury having dropped to the high forties. I'd had to harass Aureus to glamour himself before walking outside, where there were likely to be humans going to start their day, regardless of the fact that the sky was as black as it was in the dead of night. He'd complied, albeit reluctantly, and now he appeared to be wearing a perfectly-tailored suit that fit him...well, beautifully. Iona was paying more attention to him than the sky, which seemed ill-advised given that if the sun suddenly did pop out, she was going to experience a rapid, fatal case of sunburn.

"So," I said, "this has to do with what's going on in Faerie, doesn't it?"

"I would imagine so, yes," Lockwood said, squinting up at the sky, mystified.

"This is clearly the magic of the Unseelie," Aureus said, glaring over at Orianna.

Orianna glared at him. "As if I have any control over this?"

"The last time I saw clouds this thick, it was the dead of winter," I said. "And that was back in New York."

"This is no natural weather pattern," Lockwood said. "If the border has become as porous as Aureus suggests, Winter's magic could be affecting the entire Earth. Occluding the sun, lowering the temperature."

"That...that seems bad." A chill ran down my spine. "It's midsummer. In Florida. This is New York fall weather here. Maybe Florida dead-of-winter weather." I shivered again as that nasty wind came through. "Scratch that – this is getting to New York winter territory."

"Quite so," Lockwood said, still staring tentatively up at the sky. "That is the power of the magic we are dealing with, unfortunately."

"Faerie magic is nothing to be trifled with," Aureus said. "Indeed, it is a formidable force. Take comfort, Lady Cassandra, for the realm of Summer would never stoop to such levels. Our magic is pure and good, unlike those Unseelie who mean only to further themselves."

"I am standing right here, you know," Orianna said, glaring. But it was half-hearted.

"Is this Winter magic?" I asked.

"I believe so," Lockwood said.

"Then this is really serious," I said. "I mean, I realized that the boundary difficulties between the worlds was kind of a big deal for Faerie, but this? This really drives the point home, pun intended."

"What is a pun?" Orianna asked Aureus. Presumably because he'd been here longer.

"It is the bread upon which sandwich meat rests,"

Aureus said, so very confidently. "A firm foundation for excellence."

"This changes things for your other problem, too," Iona said, pointing at the sky. "When the sun's away..."

"The vampires will play?" I asked. Great. My mouth went dry as I thought of Jacquelyn and Varycas, not to mention their minions, running amok in the streets in the middle of the day. Because I needed more problems to deal with. I pulled out my phone and opened up the weather app.

"What are you doing?" Iona asked.

"I'm acting like a true Florida resident – i.e. an old person – and checking the weather." I scrolled down to the radar, clicked it–

And saw the entire state of Florida was under dense cloud cover. "Looks like we're not the Sunshine State today."

"We must go back to that blasted pixie, demand that he tell us more," Orianna said. "His is the only real direction we've had, and if he was hiding anything from us, we should find him and wring it out of him like water from a cloth."

That was enough to make me uncomfortable. I looked away, closing my eyes tight as I warred with my fatigue, trying to figure out my priority: Xandra or the Faerie problem?

Xandra was out there, somewhere, confused, experiencing her new un-life as a vampire. She could be hurting someone even now, undeterred by the shiny orb of light that should have been rising into the sky as we spoke.

But because of this Fae problem...it wasn't, and who knew if it would be anytime soon? Heck, the temperature had dropped furiously in just the last few hours. If it continued that trend, by nightfall Florida would be a lifeless icebox, like an expansion franchise of the Arctic circle right here in Tampa.

When I thought about it that way, my course seemed clear.

"I think we have to deal with the magic first," I said. "I don't like the idea of vampires running around, or leaving Xandra to her own devices, but the only way to really prevent that is by making this winter problem go away. So, much as I hate to channel Olaf...we need to bring back summer."

"Huzzah," Aureus said. A golden sword appeared in his hand and he thrust it into the sky. "Let us ride."

"Yes," Iona said, looking at him in his lovely suit. "Let's do that."

I nearly jumped as my pocket vibrated, phone going bonkers. I fished it out, and looked down at the caller ID as the chill wind cut through again, and I shivered.

But not because of the cold.

Because of the caller.

It was Xandra's mom.

22

"Hello?" I answered tentatively.

"Oh, so you decide to answer me now, do you?" Xandra's mom said. "How convenient...now that you've fled."

I blanched. "Um, Mrs. Stewart, I'm sorry, but I have no idea what you're–"

"Do not patronize me, girl." Her tone was as icy as the wind, which chose that moment to pick up and nearly bowl me over. As if this conversation wasn't already half-doing that job. My knees felt weak, unsteady, and whether that was down to tiredness or the cold was an open question. Either way, shorts had been a bad choice.

"What happened, Mrs. Stewart?" I asked as calmly as I could. Then a startling thought hit me, followed by the sensation that I had just been dropped into a dunk tank of ice water. "Mrs. Stewart, did someone show up at the house tonight?"

"Don't play dumb, missy," Mrs. Stewart snapped. "I know that you broke into Xandra's room."

I looked at Iona, eyes wide. She was glaring at the phone in my hand. Mrs. Stewart wasn't exactly being quiet with her snipes. Everyone could probably hear. Maybe even Lock-wood's neighbors.

"How dare you? I have never met someone who so dishonored the dead. How could you?"

"Mrs. Stewart, I–"

"What were you looking for, hmm? Perhaps something of yours that you just *had* to have? Or maybe it was some-thing of my daughter's, something that you had eyed on one of your many nights staying here, under our roof, dragging our daughter into Lord knows what–" The words caught in her throat as she tried to stifle a sob.

"I promise you, I would never do that," I said.

"You dragged her into terrible things," her mother said. Her voice was tight and croaky, as if she had been crying. I wouldn't have been surprised if she had been. The funeral had taken place a little over twelve hours before. "You and those...*friends* of yours."

"What did you see, Mrs. Stewart? This is very impor-tant," I said.

"My daughter is dead, Cassandra. Because of *you*. Wasn't that enough for you? Why must you come and torment her parents? What is your goal? What do you have to gain?"

The lump in my throat was growing bigger. It was Xandra. It had to be.

"What did this person do?" I asked. "Did they take anything? Or–"

"I don't know, you tell me," said Mrs. Stewart. "Did you take anything?"

I muted the call, and looked up at Lockwood. "Lock-wood, we need to get to Xandra's. And fast."

He nodded, beckoning to his car, parked in the driveway. I started walking as I unmuted it. "Mrs. Stewart, this is very important. Did you let someone into your house?"

"It was a cruel trick, Cassandra. Impersonating my daughter like that."

"Mrs. Stewart, can you please answer my question?"

"All I wanted was everyone to be happy. I wanted to see her grow, to get married, to have grandchildren. But now that dream is gone. It's gone."

"Hold on, Mrs. Stewart. I am going to come over and help you figure this out."

"Don't come back, you–"

I hung up. That conversation was going nowhere fast. Besides, I'd just plead bad cell service if she brought it up. "I think Xandra managed to get into her house," I said, hurriedly getting into Lockwood's car. "Her mom was shocked, invited her in, maybe, then...I dunno. Thought the better of it, figured I was playing a prank for...some reason." Malicious, no doubt. But it was hard to be mad at Mrs. Stewart. Her baby was dead.

And I was to blame.

"We'll be there in minutes," Lockwood said, peeling out and leaving an inch of rubber on the road as he floored it. I hung on, listening to the Faeries bickering in the back, Iona sandwiched between them, my thoughts on what Xandra was doing–

And what she might do next.

23

We made it in minutes, and I burst out of the car before Lockwood had even stopped, my shoes slapping at the front walk, the wind beating at me and threatening to bowl me over with its vicious, icy force. I reached the front porch and pounded, furiously, on the knocker, the sound probably threatening to wake half the neighborhood.

I didn't care. My throat tightened as I stood there, heart hammering almost as loud as the knocker.

"Are you all right, Cassandra?" Lockwood was only a step behind, exuding patience now that he was awake. Iona had remained in the car with the Fae, presumably to keep peace between our representatives of Summer and Winter. I doubt she'd realized I noticed her tip onto Aureus each time Lockwood went hard around a corner. Oddly, she did not do the same to Orianna on her other side when we cornered in the opposite direction.

Mrs. Stewart flung the door open after my second round of frenzied knocking. She was fully dressed in dark clothes that – for a brief second – I'd mistaken for her funeral attire. It was far less formal, I realized at second blush.

"I told you not to come here," she said, her dark eyes narrowing. Her dark hair was pulled in a severe knot behind her head, and for a wild second thought that the chopsticks in her hair were stakes like mine.

"Mrs. Stewart, I'm sorry," I said. "Whatever happened, it was not me. Can you please tell me what you saw?"

"Ditched your costume, I see," she said.

"What did this Xandra look alike do, Mrs. Stewart?" I asked. "And please, can you tell me the whole story, and just for a moment consider the possibility that it wasn't me who did...whatever this was?"

Mrs. Stewart chewed on the inside of her lip. "You swear to me you didn't do this?"

"I've been elsewhere all night," I said, and she seemed to take me in for the first time – my haggard, weary look, the bags around my eyes. "I swear to you, this was not me. Now, please – tell me what happened?"

After a long moment of consideration, she said, "A ghost, then."

My heart skipped a beat. "A ghost?"

"Xandra's ghost."

"Then why did you think it was me?" I said.

"Because ghosts aren't real," Mrs. Stewart snapped. Her cheeks were flushed.

"All right, calm down. Can I make you some tea? Maybe something to eat? When did you sit down last?"

"I don't need your help. I need–" She choked on a sob, as if unwilling to let me see her weak.

"Where is your husband?" I asked before she could bite my head off again.

"He left," she said. "He had been putting off work for

days. And it's not as if he's sleeping lately, so he decided to get an early start."

"So you were home alone when she showed up?" Her face paled as the casual mention of her deceased daughter coming home. "Tell me the whole story, top to bottom. What time was it?"

Mrs. Stewart glowered at me, crossing her arms. "I already told you. *She* showed up here, rang the doorbell. I answered it, and..."

"And what?"

She averted her eyes. "I...fell."

"In surprise?" I said. "That's not that strange."

"No, I fell and hit my head and then I...passed out." She seemed to be laboring to get the story out, and still glared at me with resentful eyes.

My skin crawled. "Did you invite her inside?"

"I don't know," she said sullenly. "I thought it was my daughter, I thought I was dreaming. I tried to embrace her, but when I touched her, her skin was so icy cold, and her eyes were so..." She recoiled a little, clutching her hand to her heart. Without really thinking about it, I reached out and grabbed her. I tilted her neck to the side before she had a chance to shove me away. "What in the world are you doing?" she exclaimed, pushing me back.

"Checking for bite marks," I said, relief spreading through me.

"Why in the world would she have bitten me?" She was looking at me like I was an idiot of the highest order. Which was fair, I thought. Because when would be the right time to tell her that her daughter was a vampire? "I fell and hit my head because I saw a ghost. Of my daughter. My *only* daughter."

"Can we come and take a look around, Mrs. Stewart?" I said.

Mrs. Stewart lifted her head, but it looked as if it took a lot of strength, as if it weighed a ton. The anger was gone from her face, and there was just deep sorrow there instead. "Fine," she said, defeated. She turned and walked toward the kitchen, dragging her feet.

I paused and beckoned back to the car. It took a moment, but I caught Iona's eye. She'd been talking – very animatedly – to Aureus. When she saw me, she nodded, and started to get out, accidentally toppling into Aureus's lap a time or three. I just shook my head and followed Mrs. Stewart inside.

"A least her mother was unharmed," Lockwood said, *sotto voce*, trailing me in. "That is good news for us. A wakening vampire is an unpredictable creature."

Iona made it to the threshold at that moment. "Can I come in?" She peered at us, and Mrs. Stewart, who gave her a gentle wave in. With that, she crossed right over. Mrs. Stewart really didn't even give her a glance.

The thought turned my stomach. She didn't know not to invite a vampire into her house, and she'd invited potentially the most dangerous one she could have right on in.

"Her room," I said to Iona, pointing up the stairs.

"Let's start there," Iona said.

"Mrs. Stewart," I called, peeking into the kitchen, where Xandra's mother had wandered. "We're going to check Xandra's room real quick, all right?'"

She had seated herself at the table in front of a cup of tea. No steam was coming from it. Her gaze darkened as she stood, the weakness she'd exhibited moments earlier fading now that I'd apparently provoked her. "No, you will not."

"Whatever, you open the door, I'll go in," Iona said. "We don't have time to be dealing with a grieving mother–"

"You've got to understand how hard this is on her–" I said.

"Harder than teeth in your jugular?" Iona's amber eyes were hard and slitted. She was past her bedtime, clearly.

Steeling my nerves, I walked around the corner and down the hall to the first door on the left. There was a little sticker there of a blue cat with wings. We'd gotten it together at the comic book store out of one of the quarter machines. She loved it so much she slapped it on there as soon as we had gotten home.

Lockwood and Iona took up positions on either side of the door, then looked at me.

"Would you like me to go in first?" Lockwood asked softly.

"No." I shook my head. That felt wrong, somehow. "This is something that I should do."

He nodded solemnly.

"Leave her room alone," Mrs. Stewart called, trailing behind. "I haven't been in there since – since –"

I pushed the door open.

The room was kind of a mess, but Xandra's room had never been the neatest. Sacks of manga lay on the floor in front of her overstuffed bookshelf, five or six half empty bottles of water sat on her bedside table. The walls were lined with posters. There was a slight hint of her perfume in the air, the tropical one from Bath and Body Works. She always smelled like sunshine and coconuts. Her favorite stuffed rabbit lay on her bed as if she had just gotten up to get ready for school.

On the wall beside her bed were pictures of us...at the beach, at the mall, at her mom's noodle shop. There was one of us with Derrick and Gregory after beating them in putt-putt golf. And the one we took with Laura at the farmer's market; Laura had treated us all to snow cones.

"I...I can't do this," I whispered. "I–"

"It's all right," Lockwood said just as softly, reassuringly. "We are right here with you."

Everything in this room had belonged to her. Everything that told me, until very recently, she was a thriving, living teenage girl. Her hairbrush. Her dry-erase board filled with appointments and dates and birthdays. Her blankets that lay in a tangled heap at the foot of the bed.

"Wow, she really tore this place apart," Iona said.

"Yeah, no," I said. "This is pretty much how it looked all the time." Still...there was no sign of *her*.

It was dark in the room, the only light spilling in from down the hall. It was cold in here, and felt lifeless.

"So what do we look for?" I asked. "Or are we at yet another dead end?"

"I don't know," Iona said. "It's not like she would come in and picked up any specific item. She'd be hazy, curious. Not looking for any particular thing, maybe just a feeling–"

A muffled *thump* came from somewhere in the room. I froze, my heart starting to beat faster, drumming against my eardrums. I turned to look at Iona, then Lockwood. The looks on their faces told me they'd heard it too.

The bed. It had come from there. I dropped to a knee, bending low to look–

"Cassie, don't–" Iona said.

But I'd already lifted the bed skirt.

A pair of orb-like eyes greeted me, glinting the dark.

The gasp didn't even make it out of my mouth before I was bowled over by an angry, frightened vampire.

24

There were stars in my eyes that I was furiously trying to blink away. I'd hit my head on the bookshelf when I'd gotten flung across Xandra's messy room. The funny thing was?

It wasn't even Xandra who'd thrown me.

It was Iona, who was grappling with Xandra even now. Both of them were growling, snarling, gone full vampire right here in the semi-dark of Xandra's anime-glutted room. Fangs were flashing, fingernails were bared, and black blood was already going everywhere.

I never thought I could be afraid of Xandra, but...I was.

They moved so fast they were like a blur, as if trying to remind me why meddling in the affairs of vamps as a human was a potentially-lethal proposition. The two of them slammed into the far wall as Lockwood retreated, dragging an open-mouthed Mrs. Stewart away from the door.

They smashed to the ground and rolled around, a blur of silvery blonde and lilac.

"What in the world is going on?" Mrs. Stewart cried from

out in the hall.

"Stay back," Lockwood said, just out of my sight. "You are in grave danger–"

Xandra snarled, an unearthly, inhuman sound. Somehow, Iona managed to throw her to the ground, pinning her by her neck, having pulled a stake from who knew where. She rammed it against the side of Xandra's neck – curious placement, I thought, even in the fog of my head injury – and said, "Settle down, anime kitty," her voice tinged with anger.

Xandra reacted as most of us would to having a sharp object at her neck and being told to calm down; she gnashed her teeth up at Iona, pale purple hair shaking.

I could barely look at her without my heart crumbling to pieces again. "Xandra, please. I know that you have to be somewhere in there. Your mom is here and she's worried sick."

Xandra lifted off the ground like a rocketship with an incredible shove, taking both her and Iona into the ceiling. Plaster caved in as they crashed into it, and the two of them resumed the fight in midair, twisting and turning as they came down. I jumped sideways into the closet as they came slamming down right where I'd been sitting.

"Xandra, you are safe, it's okay," I said to the blurry, twisting mass of them. "We're here for you. You can come with us, get some rest–"

They parted and suddenly I could see them clearly. With a jolt I realized Iona was injured. Badly. Xandra was pure fury, unbound, and Iona was trying to hold back. Constantly being on the defense...it had gotten her hurt. Black blood ran down her arm from three deep gouges near her shoulder. A trickle of it came down the back of her neck as well.

I reached up into my hair for a stake...and found

nothing.

A bang came from the hall, and suddenly Orianna and Aureus burst into the room, their long shadows stretching in. "Lady Cassandra, are you all right?" Aureus shouted.

Xandra's gaze darted up. She was on top of Iona, digging her claws in. Taking in the newcomers with a single look, I saw pure animal calculation for only a second.

Then she leapt from Iona and at the window.

Glass shattered, catching the light in a shower of sparkles, but she was already gone, a blur running into the dark.

"Lockwood!" I shouted.

"Already on it," he said, and I heard him leave – down the hall and out the front door.

"What was that sound?" Mrs. Stewart cried from out in the hall. "If you broke anything of hers, I'll have your–"

Iona staggered to her feet, clutching at her arm that was bleeding. There was a gash across her collarbone, and a tear in the leg of her jeans. It was as if she had been attacked by a bear, only worse. She tripped, but Aureus was there to catch her. "Lady Iona, you are looking rather pale, and your wounds...they are grave."

"No grave today," Iona said with a faint smile. My stomach twisted over on itself as I got a whiff of the acrid tang of the vampire blood.

Mrs. Stewart was trying desperately to get into Xandra's room, but Orianna was holding her back at the door. "You defiler, you dishonorable–"

I couldn't get the image of Xandra flailing out of my mind. She wouldn't even listen to me, wouldn't look at me. She'd torn Iona up without remorse or feeling.

She was dangerous. She was going to hurt someone.

I was going to have to kill her all over again.

25

I stumbled off the porch and onto the lawn. Lockwood and Orianna were already out there. I could sense something different in the air, a chill that transcended the normal Florida weather. A stream of bitter curses from Mrs. Stewart trailed us out, something in her native language that I didn't really want translated.

"I heard shouting," Lockwood said, wings fluttering in the lamp light as he landed. "I take it we overstayed our welcome?"

"If we ever had any welcome at all." I was starting to get a headache right behind my eyes.

Aureus came fluttering down the steps with Iona in his arms like a princess he had swept off her feet. She certainly was peering up at him as if that were the case. "The lady of the castle has ordered our removal." Gingerly, he let Iona down. When she couldn't stand, I reached out and put an arm around her waist to prevent her falling.

"Any luck finding her?" I asked.

Lockwood shook his head.

"We need to get Iona some medical attention," I said. "Or just blood, I suppose."

A sword appeared in the hand of the White Knight, and he looked down at Iona. "Tell me where your enemies are, Lady Iona, and I shall slay them and bring you their blood."

Iona *swooned.* "Be still my heart," she said. "Oh, wait. It has been for like half a century."

"Glad to see your humor is still intact," I said. Oh, for Pete's sake. I looked down, and noticed a stain of vampire blood on my shirt and shorts. Great. I was never going to get that out of these. Mill was the only one that had any idea about how to do that, and...well, I didn't think it would go over all that well for me to call him up and ask if he could give me laundry tips. "I guess we are back at square one, aren't we?"

Lockwood nodded. "Unfortunately, yes. Xandra is gone, and we still have no idea what to do about...this." He pointed up to the sky.

"I'm going to need to change my clothes, at the very least," I said.

Iona glared at me. "Sorry that my injury is such an inconvenience."

"That's not what I meant," I said. "I was talking about the shorts given we're rapidly moving toward subzero temps. Seriously, I'm about to have to break out the New York winter coat. You know how often I've needed that in Florida? Never." I pawed at the black blood across my front. "Still, while I'm at it, it won't hurt to shed this style. I look like I've been changing oil pans."

"So, back to your house it is, then?" Lockwood asked.

Mrs. Stewart's curses were getting louder; she was coming toward the porch, and I felt a need to flee. "Yes," I said, spurring them all into motion. "Back to my house." I headed for Lockwood's car, trying to keep my head down. "As quickly as possible."

26

M y dad's face when we came dragging in was the sort of thing every good – or even half-decent daughter dreads. He'd just started to smile when he saw me enter, but it faltered as he noticed the copious black blood staining my clothes and then caught sight of Lockwood carrying Iona in behind me, followed by Orianna and Aureus. He adjusted his glasses. "Rough night?"

I smiled apologetically at him. "Iona is hurt. Could you take a look at her for us?"

He looked down at his freshly pressed shirt. He'd been buttoning his cufflinks. "Alright, give me a second." Should have gone with the scrubs, Dad.

Lockwood carried her into the living room while I hurried to the laundry room to get some of our junk towels. When I returned to the living room, Lockwood was standing there patiently, holding Iona as if she were no heavier than a doll. Iona, for her part, looked more bored than anything. I stretched the towels out over the couch before Lockwood laid her down on it.

Dad came back downstairs, carrying our first aid kit that

was the size of a tackle box, dressed in an old T-shirt. "All right, Iona, let's take a look," he said, kneeling beside the couch. He snapped on some rubber gloves before examining the cut on her collarbone. "How are you feeling?"

"I'm okay," she said. "In a lot of pain, but that's just part of the game when you're hanging around with Cassie."

I decided to ignore that jab.

He pulled some gauze out of the kit and dabbed it with alcohol. I didn't have the heart to tell him vampires didn't get infections. "What did this to you? Werewolf?"

Iona glanced up at me.

I sighed. "Xandra."

Dad stopped, looking up at me.

I nodded. "Yeah." What else could I say?

"Well, other than helping you get cleaned up a bit and bandaged, there isn't really much I can do for a vampire," Dad said. "Blood will solve it, right?"

Iona looked at Lockwood. "Would you mind terribly going to my house to get some? It's in the fridge. I just picked up a fresh batch yesterday."

Lockwood nodded, and headed for the door.

Orianna, who was hovering near the kitchen island fluttered over to him. "Can I come, too?"

"No, I wish to go alone," he said, then after a moment's hesitation, "and I would rather not commit murder."

Right. That made perfect sense to me.

I left Dad to work and headed for the kitchen. The rich smell of a fresh pot of coffee was brewing, and I poured a cup to help keep my eyes from dropping closed. There was a real tug-of-war going on with my lids, and I felt like I was losing.

When I came back, Dad had finished up and was snapping his gloves off. "That's about all I can do," he said.

Aureus and Orianna had vanished. Which was probably not good.

"Thanks, Dad," I said, and gave him a kiss on the cheek as he passed. He smiled, said nothing, and headed to his bedroom. I watched Iona for a few minutes; she'd fallen asleep on the couch while he'd bandaged her. Must have been nice.

I wandered through the house, looking for the others. I found Orianna in my bed, asleep. That caused me a flash of irritation as I gathered a change of clothes more suited to the sudden precipitous drop in the mercury. Still, I tried not to wake her, and succeeded in spite of slamming a couple drawers with a little too much gusto. What can I say? I was jealous.

Wandering back downstairs, I found Mom still studying files in the chair in the corner of her room. She didn't move when Dad shut the door to the garage, and I heard the low, mechanical rumble through the house as he raised the garage door to leave. She was wearing her bathrobe, and there was a greasiness to her hair that made me wonder how many times she had run her sweaty hands through it.

The files were all open, stretched across the floor, and one sitting on her lap. She was tapping a pencil against it.

"Hey, Mom," I said, leaning heavily on the door frame.

She jumped a little when I spoke. "Oh, hi, sweetie." She gave me a weak smile. "I didn't hear you come in."

Didn't hear the parade of mythical creatures I brought home? Didn't hear Dad come in and change out of his dress shirt and grab his first aid kit? I wondered if she hadn't been dozing herself.

I knelt in front of her, and, deciding she needed my coffee more than I did, pushed it into her hands. "Take one, call me in the morning."

"So much like your dad," she said, tired eyes showing a hint of fleeting amusement. She took a sip, then blanched. "Too much. You're drinking it black, now?"

"Oh," I said. "Honestly, I just needed the energy hit." Who had time for cream and sugar?

"I worry about you," she said, lifting the mug and inhaling deeply. She let out the breath slowly and turned to look at me. "Any luck with Xandra?'

"Sort of," I said. "We found her, but she managed to get away again."

"I'm sorry, sweetie." Her eyes kept flitting back to the pages in front of her.

"Anything new?" I asked tentatively, blowing on the hot coffee. I doubted she'd drink it without cream and sugar, but personally, I seemed to gain sustenance just from smelling the stuff.

She sighed. "No. That's the problem with digging yourself a deep hole. There are no easy ways out unless someone offers you a ladder."

"Well, there's one in the garage." No laughs, there. The lump in my throat grew larger. "I'm sorry, Mom."

Mom shook her head. "Look, Cassie, I can't blame you for the choices I made. And I know all this stuff, from Byron to present, has been out of your control."

"I could have done things differently," I said. "I could have let Laura...die, I guess–"

"Ugh," she said, rolling her eyes. "So much like your dad. No, you couldn't. You could not sit aside, knowing what you knew, and let Laura die. Let our family and friends back in New York face the consequences for your actions." She shook her head slowly. "Believe me, I'm smarting more than a little from the blowback myself, but I know this – you could no more have stood aside and let events take shape, let people die, than your father could just walk past someone dying on the sidewalk. You're not the sort to spectate when you see something go wrong that you can help with, Cassie." She brushed a hand against my cheek. "It's a noble quality, as aggravating as it is to the lawyer in me. Desire to limit our liability and all that."

"I wish I could have limited some liabilities," I said softly. "I think I've picked up a few too many."

"Speaking as someone who deals with it all day long," she said, looking me tiredly in the eye, "if you don't have a liability or two, are you really living? Keep doing the right thing, sweetie." She turned her head to the window shades, then looked at the clock. "Kind of dark out for this hour, isn't it?"

"Yeah," I said, suddenly quite uncomfortable.

Her frown deepened. "Is there a storm warning?"

"Sort of," I said. "Maybe. Kind of."

She slowly turned her face to look at me, and her eyebrows were knitted suspiciously. "Is it my imagination or have you become a worse liar in these last few months?"

"I'm out of practice," I said defensively, and got to my feet. "Also, I wasn't lying. Just...not offering."

She groaned. "What do you know that you don't want to tell me?"

"That the weather is the result of some sort of upheaval in the land of Faerie," I said. "Which I may or may not have some part in–"

"Cassie," she said in a low, slow groan, burying her head in her hands. "Now you're accruing liability interfering in other lands? Magical realms?"

"Having partaken in their legal system," I said, "I don't think I'm *liable*, exactly." She gave me a hard look. "They seem to think I'm a hero, so I'm probably getting the opposite of liability." I searched for the word, but frowned, because I couldn't come up with anything. "What would that be, exactly?"

"Assets," my mother said grumpily.

"Okay, I don't really have any of those," I said, "unless you want to count a couple of Fae helpers who aren't really helping much presently."

"Halt, stranger! Who are you, and why do you seek to pass into the lands of the Lady Cassandra?" Aureus's voice rang out from the front lawn.

"Oh, look," Mom said, "it sounds like one of your non-assets is haranguing whoever is coming to the front door right now. Hopefully it's not the mailman."

"Please, the mailman doesn't get out of bed until midday," I said, pulling back the curtain a hair. My eyebrows rose in surprise when I saw who it was, though. "Huh." And I hurried to the front door, leaving Mom behind, shaking her head.

"Who is it?" Iona groaned from the couch. She made no move to get up, though.

"Your future boyfriend is blocking the doorbell," I said, hustling for the front door.

"Be nice to him," Iona called from the living room couch. "He doesn't know any better...and he's so very pretty."

"Pretty much a pain in my ass," I grumbled, jerking the front door open. Aureus's perfectly-coiffed blond locks greeted me, obstructing my view of the shaggy, blond-haired boy standing just beyond him. At the sound of the door opening, Aureus turned, and I said, "Stand down, White Knight. I know this guy." And to my guest I said, "Hey, Derrick. Come to visit the circus?"

27

"So, Derrick," I said, staring out my front door past the long-haired, muscled Fae guarding my front step to the shaggy-haired blond classmate who'd just shown up, unexpectedly. "I was not expecting to see you again. And so soon."

"Who were you expecting?" he said, looking around, as if this mystery person was going to jump out of the bushes at him. Maybe Aureus had already done that. He was pointing his sword squarely at Derrick's chest; surprisingly, Derrick seemed quite mellow about this.

"At this point," I said, "honestly, I'm half-expecting the Queen of Summer to come leaping out at me, yell curses at me for being an interfering Iron Bearer, and then–"

"No, Lady Cassandra," Aureus said, shaking his head furiously. "The glorious Queen of the Seelie would never do such a thing." He raised his hand, the Summer Court star tattoo visible upon his wrist. "Such treatment is reserved for enemies, not a champion such as yourself."

Derrick looked at me with a slightly raised eyebrow, and

mouthed, "Champion?" at me. I shook my head; better not to ask.

"So," I said, instead, "what brings you to my doorstep at this, uh..." I looked at the sweeping darkness all around. "...hour? What time is it?" I asked, hoping Iona would hear me.

"Time for you to get a watch," she called from inside. "Or to face me in the direction of a clock if you want me to function as timekeeper for you."

"It's nine o'clock," Derrick said. "In Florida. On a summer day." He gestured vaguely to the all-consuming darkness around us. "I've been through hurricanes, Cassie, plural – and they don't turn the sky this dark. What is this?" He turned his attention to Aureus, and gently turned aside the sword at his chest. Aureus let him. "And what is this? Don't get me wrong, I already like him better than Mill–"

"Do you own a mill as well, Lady Cassandra?" Aureus asked, turning to me. "If so, I will need to summon assistance from Summer to protect your holdings. Perhaps some pixies of my acquaintance. Formidable guards in spite of their stature." He turned thinly-slitted eyes to the sky. "They would be very useful against these dread white birds that hang about. I sense a baseness from them akin to the Avara back in Faerie."

"Is anything he just said making any kind of sense to you?" Derrick asked, peering around him.

"Avara are humans that stumble into Faerie and are turned by the greedy desire of their hearts into pigs," I said, feeling very much like Captain America in that I understood that reference. So worldly, too, for a girl who hadn't even graduated high school yet.

"I suspect the same magic at work with these," Aureus said, pointing at Gregory's lawn next door. A couple seagulls were there, eyeing us. Laura, two doors down, fed them, which was why they were lurking. "Foul creatures."

"The gulls?" Derrick asked, then, apparently not finding any argument added, "Agreed."

"'Gulls,'" Aureus said, turning the word over in his mouth. "Yes. I hate them already."

"You and everyone else in Florida," I said. "Aureus – can you excuse us for a moment? Derrick and I need to talk."

"Certainly," Aureus said with a curt nod. "I intend to start on a moat to protect your lands in any case. Orianna informed me of the presence of a 'shovel' in the motor stables that will allow me to commence work immediately." He started toward the garage.

"Wait – whoa!" I caught him by the shoulder. "No moats." I shook my head very seriously. "Dad will have a cow."

"You have cows as well?" Aureus stared at me in great concentration. "I'm going need more pixies," he mumbled.

"No moat," I said, unable and unwilling to explain myself at this hour or with my current lack of sleep, frankly. "Besides, most of my villains can fly or just leap over it. Think of the seagulls."

"Accursed gulls," Aureus said, eyeing them once more. "You make great sense, Lady Cassandra. You are as wise as you are beautiful. I will defend your lands in spite of these encumbrances. You can count on me."

"I would like to count on him," Iona sighed as I led Derrick inside and shut the door behind us, leaving Aureus patrolling the front lawn. "To twenty-one, to be specific."

I understood that reference, too, and I wished immediately that I didn't. "So," I asked Derrick, who looked immensely uncomfortable, "what brings you by this morning? Status update? We're working on the weather thing, albeit slowly. And as you can see, we're all stocked up on crazy, so that's covered."

"Oh," Derrick said, "no. Don't get me wrong, I'm interested in weather and craziness. But I came to apologize."

I strolled into the kitchen, screwing up my face as I did so. "Apologize for what?" Coffee was calling my name. Well, actually my bed was, but coffee seemed the solution since Orianna had stolen my bed.

Derrick followed me, crisp, sure stride carrying across the kitchen. "I feel bad about how I acted last night at the gas station."

I rubbed my face with my hands, suddenly feeling a lot more tired about my life in general than I had just a few minutes before. "Wow, that was last night? Time doesn't just fly around here, it goes to light speed."

"I know that you just went through a really crappy thing losing Xandra, and I just totally blew you off." He slid his hands into his pocket. "So...I'm sorry."

"It's fine," I said. "I was kind of distracted myself, and it's none of my business who you hang out with–"

"Yeah, but you're my friend, Cassie," he said. "I shouldn't have run from you the way I did." There was something so...different about the way he was carrying himself. He was apologizing for being cowardly. But he'd been staring down the blade of a sword unflinchingly just a few minutes before.

"It's all right," I said. "Really. No big deal. I forgive you."

It was a visible relief. "Thanks," he said, a smile curling up one side of his face. "So, um, I wanted to apologize, but also..." He waved a hand around. "This darkness? Is there mojo? Voodoo? Moodoo?" He paused, thinking. "That sounds like a cow demon thing, actually."

"There is mojo moodoo going on, yeah," I said. "Or maybe just doodoo."

"I thought so," he said. "Can I help?"

I blinked at him. "You know, it's not a video game, Derrick."

He looked at me dead on. "I know."

My brow furrowed as I looked at him. When the vamps had attacked us all after the play a week or so ago – was that only a week ago? – he had been completely frozen in fear. He'd said after Xandra died how useless he felt, how helpless he was.

Well, here he was, making good on that. And I needed help, whether or not I wanted to admit it. I was facing threats on all sides. "I should let you know that it isn't just the Faerie weather stuff we're dealing with," I said. "We're also looking for another vamp."

"Looking for another vamp?" he asked. "Some terrifying badass that drinks blood straight out of the skull?"

"Ew," Iona said, which I felt was a measure of how disgusting Derrick's proposal had been, given our sole vampire had just voted it down.

"Worse," I said. "Xandra."

Derrick paled. "That is worse."

"She's out there," I said. "Newly raised, fumbling around in the dark. We don't think she's killed yet, but...it's just a matter of time."

"Oh, man," Derrick said. "So you need all the help you can get?"

"Every bit of it," I said, "provided it's not the kind that's a, uhm..." and I thought of my mom, "...liability."

Derrick just nodded, not taking that as the insult he might have only a week ago. "I'll make myself useful. Go help that suited Englishman out there with guarding the yard." He started toward the door. "And Cassie?" His eyes met mine, and there was a warmth in his pale blue eyes, the green in them standing out somehow even more right now. "Thanks for letting me help."

"Sure," I said, holding the coffee pot in my hand as I listened to Derrick retreat softly to the front door, and walk out it. Wind blew through, sudden, heavy, and cold, and I shivered even with the warm carafe beside my fingertips.

Something had changed about him. I just couldn't put my finger on it.

———————

28

Lockwood showed up a few minutes later, somehow passing the perimeter that Aureus and Derrick were manning in the yard without any shouts. Clearly my White Knight was slipping. He walked in carrying a small red and white cooler, blustery wind howling in with him. "Where is Iona?" he asked softly.

I pointed to the couch where Iona's hand appeared, waving him over. I heard footsteps on the stairs and turned to look, expecting to see Mom. But it was Orianna, rubbing her eyes with the back of her hand. She squinted in the bright can lights of the kitchen.

"Why is Aureus talking loudly to someone about the gull of the seas?" Orianna asked, voice scratchy. She didn't have her glamour on, and her weariness showed.

"He's discovered the local flying rats," I told her. "Apparently he isn't all that fond of them."

Iona appeared at that very moment, fresh as a daisy and clutching a pint of O-neg that had been drained down to the dregs, residue staining the clear plastic. "Mind if I borrow some clothes?" she asked. "Forgot to tell Lockwood to get me some while he was out."

"Sure, go ahead," I said.

She trudged up the stairs, black stains clinging to the holes in her shirt and pants. I could see hints of smooth, unblemished skin beneath, between the globs of oily vampire blood.

"Cassie," Orianna said, "when she's done, would you mind if I used some of your small nose glamour?"

"My...what?" I said.

"That pretty bottle that tried to attack me," she said. "It smelled rather nice. And it has been days since I had a chance to bathe. It seems unlikely that I will have a chance to again with the lack of waterfalls here."

"We do have showers you know," I said, leaning on the counter. I was debating about dragging out a box of cookies, but I didn't feel like answering questions about them.

"Storms?" Orianna said, her brow furrowing. "I know I'm Winter Fae, but I have limits to the cold I'm willing to endure while bathing."

"No, that's not what I meant–"

More footsteps behind me heralded the arrival of Mom, wearing her bathrobe and slippers. She walked right past me, heading straight for the cream and sugar.

"Hey, Mom?" I asked. "Could you show Orianna how the shower works?"

Mom set down the sugar, looking like she wanted to ask some questions. In the end, though, she just stirred her coffee and said, "Sure, dear. Let's introduce you to the magic of the human world." She shepherded Orianna toward the stairs, making a face as she did so. "And also...deodorant."

"Deodorant? That sounds mythical."

I sipped my coffee slowly for the next few minutes,

rubbing my eyes and leaning on the kitchen counter. A slow, rhythmic breathing caught my attention, and I tracked it to my dad's easy chair in the corner of the family room, where Lockwood lay unconscious, feet up, head tilted sideways, making something just short of a snoring sound.

Trying to control a giggle through my exhaustion, I took another sip of my coffee. Brave Lockwood, showing up even though he was exhausted.

A scream from upstairs jarred me back awake just as Iona was coming down in jeans and one of my T-shirts. She tensed, spinning on the bottom step, ready to charge back up–

"Cassandra!" My mom came down, bathrobe soaked. "She has wings. *Wings*. And she splashed *everywhere*. She was like a dog, shaking them out."

I smiled apologetically at her, cupping my coffee. "Sorry, Mom."

She huffed and turned toward her bedroom. "I swear, these mythical creatures you bring home...ugh."

I turned and found Lockwood hovering over my dad's easy chair, his eyes wide, all vestiges of sleep gone. "Sorry, Lockwood. We didn't mean to wake you."

"That's quite all right," he said, voice weary. It was only quite all right in the sense a British person might mean it. Which was to say many things would fit in the rubric of "quite all right." An appendectomy. Your house burning down. The cast of *Jersey Shore* throwing a party in your backyard. He settled back down in the chair, wings disappearing beneath his glamour. A few seconds and he was breathing slowly again, though his eyes were open and pointed at the TV, which was muted but still playing. "Hm. It appears the human news has caught on, at least a bit."

I found the remote next to me on the counter and

unmuted it. The weather anchor, a jovial older man, was doing his bit. "It's a strange one out there, folks. Temps today are projected for a low of thirty degrees, and based on the way this front is acting, I could see it going lower, like a contortionist in a limbo contest." He laughed in a folksy way. "I know, I know – this is some weird weather for summer! In fact, given our current eighty percent chance of precipitation, you might just be telling your grandkids about the great mid-summer blizzard you saw in–"

"Well, crap," I said, the little hairs on the back of my neck standing up. "Lockwood, what do you make of this?"

"Clearly the humans are noticing something is wrong," he said. "And doing their very best to keep it within the realm of reality. 'Fronts' indeed. Poor sods."

"We're all poor sods at this point," I said. "We need some guidance. What is happening? Why is Winter bleeding through into Earth? What happens next?" I took a deep breath. "How do we stop it?"

Lockwood lifted his hands in apology. "I'm sorry, Cassandra. I don't know who would have answers outside of Faerie– " My eyes grew wide. "No," he said, heading me off. "Absolutely not. We cannot go back there. I have been banished."

"Goodbye for a while is not goodbye forever," I said.

Lockwood's eyes appeared to be in danger of rolling back in his head. "Forever is in fact what banishment means. They want me gone *forever*, or they will *kill me*. Besides," and here he grimaced, "my usual path to Faerie has been closed."

"Is there no way to reopen it?" I said.

"I – I don't know," Lockwood said, rubbing his forehead. "Magic is a very fickle thing. Even if we were to cross to

Faerie, who do you imagine we could talk to that would want to speak with us?"

"The Summer Court," I said, glancing out the front window. Aureus and Derrick seemed to be speaking amiably, posted up on the front walk. "In fact, I don't think it'd be an exaggeration to say I'm much more popular there than I am here."

"Maybe if you'd stop burning things down on this planet," Iona said, leaning over the counter, "you'd be more popular." She looked way better in my clothes than I did, and I was not going to dignify that with a response. Mostly because it'd come out bitterly jealous.

This was, of course, the moment Orianna chose to make her entrance, sashaying down the stairs in my favorite top and jeans. "Uh," I said, "those are mine. Unless you're wearing a glamour...?"

"I know, I just love them," Orianna said, gushing. "I was listening to your conversation – you know there's more than one way into Faerie, right?

Lockwood stared at her with his usual lack of amusement. "What other way would you propose? Personally, I would prefer one that does not include border guards looking to separate me from my head, and so far as I am aware, such locales are few and very far between.

"When the borders are strong you're funneled to those few points, sure," Orianna said with a magical little laugh that reminded me of a cheerleader for some reason. "But the borders are weak, Lockwood. I bet the old twingates are wide open right now."

"Twingates...?" Lockwood's eyes widened. "Of course." He smacked his forehead with his palm. "The sister doors."

"I prefer the regular Doors," Iona said dryly. "Jim

Morrison was great as he was; all-female reboots tend to suck."

"What's a sister door?" I asked.

Orianna looked at me, eyes aglow. "There are objects in your world that have a twin in Faerie."

"Yes, and I know of one such door," Lockwood said. "It was sealed a long time ago, but since the veil is so thin, it is likely those locked passages are not locked any longer."

"Okay, then we need to move quickly," I said. I looked at Lockwood. "Where is this sister object?"

"It's a fountain," he said. "Downtown."

"Do we have no other option but to go and get answers directly from the source itself?" Iona asked.

"Yeah," I said. "What exactly are we hoping to get from the other side?"

Lockwood sighed. "You know I do not like the idea of going back. But if the Seelie Court can provide some current insight, we might be able to track down the problem on this side. And if the queen being deposed was just a rumor, then we can squash that and perhaps focus on whatever the real problem is. Clarity. We need it. And I struggle to know who else could provide it."

"Where does this twin door let out on the other side?" I asked. "Are we going to have to spend another week in Faerie? Or cross the land searching for the Court? Because I do not have the energy for that right now."

"It comes out in the land of Seelie," Orianna said, "in town, perhaps a furlong from the castle gates."

"That's about two football fields," Iona said. "In case you needed it translated from the old-ish."

"Short commute," I said. "I'll mark this in the plus column for this plan."

"What is the minus?" Lockwood asked.

"Potential death for you – if you come," I said. "Lack of answers, wasting time, drawing us away from what's...going on here." I meant Xandra. Of course I meant Xandra.

"What if it isn't a waste of time?" Iona asked. "What if you get all the answers you're searching for, and we have a clear idea what we need to do to fix this wintry calamity?" She fixed me with a pointed stare. "Why, then you might be able to get on with saving the day...and we can all go to bed after." She turned to look out the front window, looking at Aureus. "Which I think is something we all agree is necessary. And proper. And–"

"Nothing you are saying is proper right now," I said, pursing my lips disapprovingly.

"If I may remind you, Lady Cassandra," Lockwood said, "time moves a great deal more slowly in Faerie. We would only be gone moments from Earth. The likelihood of anything happening in our absence is minimal."

That was a fair point. Still: "What, you're on board now?"

"I would prefer not to go personally, if possible." He shrugged. "But I do not think we have another viable choice at this moment."

"Well, okay, fine" I said. "Let's say we go over there. Orianna, what could they say over there, in the Seelie Court, that would help us?"

"I almost think we need more of an update from that side of the border as much as anything." She scratched the side of her cheek. "When I arrived here, Faerie was greatly affected, but your world seemed immune." She pointed at the TV. "Clearly, that has changed. The calamity links us together somehow, but if it's showing up in Faerie first..."

"By going there, we may be seeing our future," I said. "Sort of, anyway."

She nodded. "The most troubling thing is, and I think

that the Seelie here can agree...if this continues, neither world is going to be able to survive this."

That was grim. Goosebumps appeared on my arms, and not from the cold.

"All right." My choice was clear; Xandra would have to wait. The world was hanging in the balance. "Let's go find this twin door fountain thing."

29

I t was a pretty ordinary fountain, all things considered.

Tiered in the center, with a few concentric bowls that grew larger the lower they were. Water splashed from the top, overflowing into each terrace beneath, and so on until it bubbled over into the basin at the bottom. It looked like the sort of thing you'd find in any park – and nothing like what I would've expected a mythical "twingate" to look like.

"Are you sure," I said, listening to it burble, "this is a passage to Faerie?"

Lockwood nodded. "If you were to get very close to the pillar in the center, you would see a unique design of a leaf on the topmost tier. The core of the fountain is made of a stone only found in Faerie. A similar one from Earth was incorporated into its twin in Faerie, linking the two inextricably."

We stood in the cold, the six of us – Iona, Lockwood, Orianna, Derrick, Aureus, and myself. Half of us were shivering, and that included me, stuffed into my New York winter coat. "I'll take your word for it," I said, rubbing my hands together. "Let's get this done."

"Are you cold?" Orianna asked me. She wore my shirt and jeans, no socks, no shoes, and I was pretty sure her glamour was only covering her wings and the strangeness of her fae features, not her outfit. Her skin showed no chill bumps on her forearms.

"Kind of," I said. "It isn't the worst cold I've felt, but it's the worst for Florida."

"Then you will not enjoy what I have to say next," Lockwood said. "We have to reach the center of the fountain."

I stared at dully. "We have to wade through that water? In this?"

"If you cannot fly," he said, "unfortunately, yes. I have to be touching the stone in order to cast the spell, and it has a limited range."

"Might as well get that part over with," Iona said, and clutched Aureus by the biceps. "Come on, Summer Lovin.'"

Derrick made the strangest face. "Is that a *Grease* reference?"

"She's old," I said, and immediately the wind picked up, cold and vicious, like the look Iona shot me. The fountain water was scummy, with green ick clinging to the tile at the bottom and up the side of the basin, though it was hard to tell with the ice crystals starting to form at the edges.

"I can carry one of you to the top," Aureus announced, and Iona almost flung herself into his arms. "Oh. Well, if Lady Cassandra is all right with it..."

Iona gave me a searing look, as if pressing me to make up for dogging her about her age just now. "I have gotten half clawed to death for you tonight," she said under her breath.

"Fine," I said, and shot a look at Orianna. "Can you carry m–?"

She didn't even bother to hide her brow-raising look as she gave me the once-over. "I am not. That. Strong." She flitted to the top without me, where Iona clung to Aureus, and Lockwood inspected the top of the fountain, the spray already partially occluded by ice.

There was splash to my side; Derrick was already in and wading toward the next tier.

"How did you–" I asked, watching him with my nose all curled up in disdain. I was not looking forward to this.

"I did a polar plunge in Alaska with my dad when I was a kid," he said. "This is nothing compared to that."

"Of course you did." I whimpered a little as I sank my foot into the water, biting my tongue as I suppressed a shiver racing up my spine. Goosebumps broke out on my arms as I felt the water starting to soak its way up past my knee.

Iona looked down from her position in Aureus's arms. "How bad is it?" She wore a mean little smirk.

I waded across the icy water, shivering all the way. "I feel like a snowman has got me by the l-l-l-legs," I said, teeth chatting. Reaching the second tier, I found Derrick already climbing, and soaking his upper body in the process.

Dammit. These were fresh clothes. A chunk of ice drifted across and collided with my knee, sticking there.

I grit my teeth and sucked in a breath, readying myself for the bite that was coming. I put my arms on the next tier, water rushing down around me in a fall, soaking my shirt and making me gasp in frigid, hypothermic shock. When I regained my senses, I managed to get a leg up on the next level and pull myself up against the freezing flow of water. By now, I was completely soaked and shivering, and regretted all the choices I'd ever made in life that had brought me to this terrible, awful point. Especially anything to do with Byron, and vampires, and Fae.

By the time I made it up two more tiers, my hands were shaking, balled into fists. My teeth were banging together like those wind-up chattering teeth toys. I felt like I'd never been warm in my life, and I never would be, ever again. Cold was all there was – cold today, cold tomorrow, cold yesterday and forever. I was a princess of ice, born to the freeze, and it was how I'd live, and how I'd die.

Suddenly, Lockwood was beside me, his eyes warm in the spray of the freezing cold fountain. "That is close enough, Cassandra. You needn't trouble yourself to climb any farther."

"Oh, g-g-g-good," I managed to chatter out. I plopped down, my legs already giving out anyway.

Lockwood flitted up to the next level and placed his hand in the center of the fountain. The others were there, I realized dimly – Derrick, a level below the top, on one knee in a smaller terrace than mine. Aureus still held Iona, and Orianna fluttered around a few feet behind Lockwood. With a wave of his hand, and a flash, Lockwood gave me one more look: "Are you ready, Cassandra?" he asked, voice deep with concern. I nodded, unable to produce an answer with my teeth chattering.

With a flourish, Lockwood cast his spell, and there was a flash–

And suddenly...I wasn't in Tampa anymore.

30

Traveling to Faerie was not something I would consider fun, exactly. It was like being sucked up a straw filled with disco lights and mashed potatoes, or shoved down one of those vertical water slides at high speeds where the plastic cuts up your back and your aren't even touching it for half the ride. But through a bunch of mashed potatoes.

I don't know I thought of mashed potatoes so much as I was dragged, kicked, pushed, pulled and ultimately thrown bodily into Faerie. Maybe I was hungry. Or maybe it was because whatever magic was pressing on me seemed thick and heavy, and I was being pushed right through it whether I liked it or not.

Then, just as suddenly as it began, the mashed potato thrill ride stopped.

I opened my eyes, not realizing that I had clamped them tightly shut, and looked around.

We were still standing in the fountain, and for a second I thought that the spell hadn't worked. Then I realized that the temperature of the water was no longer near-freezing.

I looked over my shoulder and gasped.

We were in Faerie, all right. I could tell because it was so unlike Earth that there was no way it could ever have been mistaken for it.

We were in a glen of some sort. There was a marble portico like the one that Lockwood and I had made our way through before, and some stone benches scattered around. A winding path led between two trees at the far side of the clearing.

It was different than I remembered it, though. Where the enormous trees had once been green and full of life, these were tired and dying. All of their leaves were littering the ground beneath their large trunks. There were faces in the bark, all of which were frozen in time, caught in an expression of pain.

Lockwood had said that the trees were living and could turn against us. I had no idea they had faces, though.

The grass was covered in frost, and the sky overhead was grey and gloomy. The air smelled of snow, and it was eerily quiet everywhere. Every movement, every splash of the water as we descended the fountain mountain could be heard, echoing around us.

"Wow," Derrick said, sloshing his way out of the fountain. "So this is Faerie."

"Terrible!" Aureus cried as he fluttered to the side of the fountain, depositing Iona on solid ground. "Things have taken a frightful turn while I was gone. This breaks my heart such that I would rather dwell with Gladys for a thousand nights than torment myself with this atramentous vision of my home."

I was surprised to see that his glamour had disappeared. He was standing there in all of his brilliance, the glow around him had returned. Iona's eyes widened when she stared at him. I had to admit, it was hard for me to look away from him as well. "It's okay," she said, patting him on the shoulder in his distress. She seemed almost sincere, save for the purr in her voice.

"What has happened to this place...?" Lockwood's voice sounded like a walk through dead leaves. His eyes caught on every surface, lingering, pain on his face. He, too, had lost his glamour. Sometimes I forgot that he was wearing one when he was on Earth. Here, though, his slate blue hair was back, hanging just above his ears, and his wings fluttered anxiously behind him. He looked younger, too, and more vulnerable. My heart ached as I watched him stare around, taking in the sight of the lands of his birth.

"Lockwood, did we make a wrong turn somewhere?" I said. "Is this Unseelie territory?"

"No," Orianna said, with grim certainty. "This is definitely Seelie land." Her golden hair was long again, hovering around her like Medusa's snakes.

"But how–"

Aureus threw himself to the ground. "Brother trees! Didst the seagulls get to you? My heart aches. I shall avenge thee!"

Lockwood walked over to the nearest trees at the edge of the clearing. He rested his palm against it, head bowing.

"I don't think I've ever seen him like this," Iona said. "I know you told me he really had blue hair, but I think I imagined it more in the Florida sense of the word, like a granny. Do you think he's okay?"

"I don't know," I said. "Lockwood is really strong, but this is his home. I can't imagine what he must be feeling to have come back from exiled to find it like this."

"My apologies," Lockwood said, withdrawing his hand

from the tree. "I never expected to find things this grim. It is...hard to take in all at once."

"It's fine," I said. "I understand how hard it is to find your home in ruins."

Lockwood gave me a sad sort of smile. "We are in a garden near the castle. If we proceed in this direction, we should reach the court shortly." He pointed behind us.

Gathering ourselves and our unhappy Seelie party members, we proceeded through the crunch of dead leaves into the quiet tree line that ringed the garden. The trees were tall and skeletal, barely stirring in the chill wind. Soon enough, they were gone, no longer blocking our view of the overcast skies and the tall buildings of the Seelie capital beyond. Even that, though, was changed.

The magnificent city of Starvale, which had once been one of the most beautiful sights I had ever laid eyes on, was a mere shadow of what it once was. The city itself had been like a rainbow of buildings situated on a floating chunk of rock, with swirling magical color below, but it was gone now, and dark. That magic had seemingly been leeched away, and all was dark and gray. The floating nature of the castle had faded, and it seemed to have settled low, as if it had sunk into the towers of the city.

Now, too, the once-glorious castle was clouded, broken, and dull. Some of the grand spires that had stretched into the sky had cracked and fallen off, and all of the floating towers beside it had disappeared completely. I waited for my vision to flicker, for the illusion of a glamour to be ripped away, but nothing happened.

This was the reality of Starvale, capital of the Seelie Fae.

"Starvale," Aureus whispered. "What has happened to the pride of our people?"

"We have to get to the castle," Lockwood said. "To the court."

"What if we get stopped on the way, though?" Orianna asked.

"I get this feeling," I said, chill and grim from the cold water still clinging to my skin, "there are not many, if any, people just waiting around in there to stop us."

"If Summer has transformed this much already," Lockwood said, "we don't have much time left."

We proceeded through the warren of cracked and destroyed buildings. Where once some houses hovered above the rest, suspended by magic, now they had fallen into crumbled ruin. Hints of frost glazed the collapsing rooftops, and the air held a bitter chill. The scent of lavender, vanilla, and coffee had once been on the breeze; now the stink of death was in the air, and I held my cold and wet sleeve to my nose and shivered, not just from the chill but from the horror in this place.

"This is incredible," Derrick whispered to me. "I get that stuff is majorly wrong, but even still..."

"This is nothing like it was last time I was here," I said. "I wish you could have seen it in all its glory, despite how crazy and terrifying the Seelie Court could be."

"No," Aureus said, then cried, "No!"

I didn't have to take more than two steps to see what he was mourning.

A guard dressed in his Paladin's armor was sprawled out on the ground. He was lying in a strange position, though, almost as if he were a statue that had been knocked over. He was crouched, almost in mid-run, and his face was frozen in pain.

"You fought bravely, brother," Aureus said, kneeling

down to examine the soldier. "We shall free you from this state, I assure you."

"I hate to say anything, since I don't know anything about the workings of Faerie," Iona said, "but just looking around there's frost on the ground, no leaves on the trees, it's cold...this has to be the Winter Court, right?"

Orianna's eyes narrowed. "Winter has not done this. I know what it looks like, but this is not Unseelie magic."

"Okay, but then what is it?" I asked. "I'm with Iona, how could this not be Winter when the whole place is, well...all it's lacking is a few Halloween decorations and the smell of pumpkin spice to be full-on autumn themed."

Lockwood was cradling his face in his hand, as if he could not bear to see any more. "We must get to the castle. There we may find the answers we seek–"

"If there are any forces of Summer remaining," I said, grabbing the back of his shirt. "They may kill you on sight."

"They will be grateful for my help," Lockwood said. "As I am one of the few they can trust that is from Earth. Regardless of what my actions caused here last time, they cannot deny that I am loyal to the Seelie."

I sighed, letting him go. "I have a really bad feeling about this."

For a few minutes, the only sound around us was the sound of our feet scraping against the ground as we trudged on. There were no bird songs, no gentle breeze meandering through the branches overhead. It was the muffled quiet of winter, surrounding us in chilled silence. The skin on the back of my neck pricked up. There was nothing and no one around.

So why couldn't I shake the sense of impending dread?

31

The castle was just as big as I remembered it. It towered over our heads as we crossed the twisted bridge to its sunken island, still hovering over the endless pit of some sort of swirling magic. Where before the glow had been blue, it now just looked like a bottomless pit of black. I tried to avoid looking over the edge for fear of vertigo, or falling.

"That's...wow, that's dark," Derrick said, apparently not so wise as me.

The guards on either side of the door were still there, ever diligent. Blue and stiff, like the one we'd seen in the streets of Starvale, but they'd frozen at their posts. Ice coated the once beautifully polished floor of the foyer in little drifts of frost.

Other Seelie were inside, also frozen. Some were seated on benches, cringing in pain; others who had been standing were on the ground just as the guard in the road had been.

The foyer was not quite as grand as I remembered it. The magical map of Faerie was no longer hovering in the center of the domed room. In fact, the pool below it was now a solid sheet of ice. In the chill, I shivered, ice forming on my wet clothes. How long did it take for hypothermia to set in?

"How could this happen?" Aureus asked. "Summer has fallen."

"It hasn't fallen yet, Aureus," Lockwood said. "All hope is not gone."

"But this magic," Aureus said, his feet dragging, "this is not just cold, Paladin. Chill exists in the heart of Summer, an utter impossibility. It is like lighting a fire in the water; this is as if the very life force of Summer is being drained."

Lockwood glared over his shoulder at Orianna.

"Do not blame this upon my people," she said, her eyes narrowing.

"I have a great deal of evidence that suggests I should," Lockwood said, grazing his fingers across the frozen surface of what must have been a painting or a mirror at some point, but was now so shrouded in ice I couldn't tell.

"Let's go a little farther," I said, trying to speak around chattering teeth. "Maybe we'll find some answers."

The halls were twisting and curving, more like a cave than a grand castle. The large, spiraling staircase that I had walked up and down during my time here was slick with ice, which clung to the underside of the stairs, hanging like thin, jagged chandeliers.

Aureus was now shivering, trying to pull his cloak closer around himself.

"Don't worry, I'll keep you warm," Iona said, drawing nearer to him.

"You are literally room temperature," I said. "And this room is *cold.*"

She glared at me, but did not deign to answer that.

"Hey, you okay?" Derrick said, coming up beside me as

we turned another corner. It was like a maze. I couldn't remember the way to the ballroom where the court was held. I was just following Lockwood, who seemed to be drifting along in numb horror. I was just drifting along numb.

"Yeah, just a little chilly," I said, trying to rub some warmth back into my arms.

"Here," he said, pulling his hoodie off.

"No, it's all right," I said. "I don't want you to freeze. I'm used to the cold–"

But he just smiled at me and wrapped his sweatshirt around my shoulders anyways.

Warm relief spread through me. It was fleece lined, warm, and I caught the faintest hint of spearmint clinging to it. "Are you sure you don't need it?"

He shook his head. "I'll be fine. Honestly, the cold feels kind of good after how hot this summer has been."

I only hesitated for another second before sliding my arms through the sleeves, relishing the warmth it provided.

Derrick slid his hands into his pockets. I watched his bare arms for signs of goosebumps that might prove that he was lying to me and just trying to be nice. Even a few minutes later, his teeth weren't chattering like mine had been. He appeared alert and ready, and strangely zen.

I was still confused by this change. He didn't look terrified, even though we were literally in an entirely new world, and a fairly dead one, at that.

In fact, he appeared almost...confident.

"We are nearly there," Lockwood said, drawing my attention from Derrick. Another few steps and he stopped, pressing a finger to his mouth, silencing the rest of us.

Beyond a set of grand double doors – though, I would swear, not nearly as grand as when last I'd been here – the grand ballroom lay. Snow fell gently from the ceiling, and great drifts covered the floor below. Icicles hung from the ceiling overhead like fixtures for some winter ball.

The balconies at either of the room stood empty, the gilded thrones on them standing unoccupied and waiting. The doors leading out to them with the stars engraved on them were closed, frosted in a sheet of sparkling ice.

"It's empty," Lockwood said. "But the queen...she should be here. She should be–"

"She was deposed," Iona said. "Or had you forgotten that?"

"A rumor is as good as a lie in the eyes of a Seelie," Lockwood said. "At least until confirmed. Still, even if she were, the king should be here, along with the other members of the court." He paced the room, leaving tracks in the snow. He'd been on Earth for so long he was forgetting to use his wings.

Orianna knelt beside another faerie that was frozen against the wall. "These faeries are not dead. But it is as if the life itself is being sapped from these poor people."

"I do not see anyone associated with the court," Aureus said, stooping to peer into the face of another fallen faerie. "Not the scribes, not the hangers-on – guards, only. The court is gone," he said voice echoing in the cavernous ballroom. "Summer is not here anymore."

32

"What has happened here?" Lockwood whispered, his voice punctuating the quiet of the frigid ballroom where once Summer had held court. Now it was a court of silence, a freezing wind whipping through and chilling my wet jeans, making me draw my borrowed sweatshirt tight to me, the hood up to keep my ears warm. "This place must have been abandoned for some time, and the guards are simply...frozen."

"Then has the Summer Queen been deposed?" Iona asked, walking in her graceful way through the piles of snow, every footstep yielding a small crunch that seemed to make Aureus blanch.

"If so, someone would, presumably, take her place," Lockwood said, "for why depose without replacing?" He turned to Aureus. "Is it possible the entire court was overthrown?"

Aureus wrung the front of his tunic, his wings becoming perfectly still. "Sir Paladin, I am afraid there is much about the court that I did not know, even before I left – which must have been long ago now, indeed. This I can say – Starvale was intact when last I was here, and there was no hint of this...madness." His voice choked off.

"You don't think our time here caused this," I asked, gesturing up at the daggers of ice dangling above our heads.

Lockwood sighed. "I do fear that we set something in motion. Sentiment here might have been like a cauldron bubbling just below the surface. One crack and it could surge free, consuming all."

"But to have it all happen without the Unseelie Court's knowledge?" Orianna asked. "This would have to be done very quietly, indeed."

Lockwood glared at her. "I am still not convinced your court is blameless."

"I realize I just got in on this whole Faerie-thing, but surely there's an explanation," Derrick said. "Maybe they had no choice but to leave because of the cold?" He waved a hand around, indicating the fallen, the ice. "It's not exactly a summer day on Sarasota beach in here, and if these are Summer fae...they have a cold tolerance, presumably?"

Lockwood frowned, shaking his head. "In spite of appearances, I'm worried that this is more of an internal matter. Something happened on the inside to–"

"Friends, I hate to be the bearer of bad news, but..." I turned and looked at Aureus, whose face had paled. "...something is amiss." He pulled his sword from the sheath at his hip.

I strained to listen. The room had been silent aside from our conversations.

Now, though, I heard a distant *thump...thump...thump.*

Lockwood's eyes narrowed as he held out his hands, summoning a bright blue orb of light. Orianna, likewise, had summoned her own spell, a swirling red mist. Iona bared her fangs, and even Derrick seemed to be at attention.

We were not alone.

33

There was a great *crack* that echoed through the room, causing the floor beneath our feet to buckle and ripple. I fell to my knees, catching my palms against the cold, snowy floor. There was another *crack*, and on the far side of the room, the floor burst open, sending broken shards of magical glass and snow in all directions.

We covered our heads, ducking as the debris fell around us. Lockwood cast a charm around us, one of his forcefields, protecting us from the largest of the pieces of debris "What could be coming up from the floor – " I started to say.

But the answer crawled up before I could finish.

Huge creatures, humanoid in shape, struggled their way up to the ballroom from somewhere below. Their fingers were jagged, and were frosted and pointed, like chunks of ice. I swallowed with a dry tongue as their heads appeared, three of them. They were flat like rocks, with glowing lumps of ice where eyes should have been. The bodies were huge, crystalline, and the cold just *breathed* off of them.

"This is a craven attack of Winter upon us!" Aureus cried, brandishing his sword. Somehow, in the commotion, he had managed to put himself between myself and the icy giants. "Do not fear, Lady Cassandra. I am here to protect you." Shuddering with cold, I didn't even have the strength left to remark on that.

"This is not Winter's doing," Orianna said, but did I detect a hint of...uncertainty?

"Orianna, I'm starting to think that your case is weak," Derrick said. "I may not know a whole lot about all this Faerie stuff, but it's pretty clear that ice behemoths and Winter seem to have a lot in common."

Orianna readied more of the red mist in her opposite hand. "They are animals, not minions of the Winter Court. The Winter Queen has no control over them."

The icy giants, now fully unfolded from the chasm on the other side of the room, let out a trio of bellowing roars that shook some of the icicles loose from the ceiling. That shattered upon the snowy ground, sending shards in all directions. I dove out of the way just as one came hurtling down from above.

"I dearly hate to agree with the Unseelie, but she is right, these are not under anyone's control," Lockwood said. "I think they have nested here in the court's absence. It would be akin to blaming the mayor for a termite mound at your home."

"I told you this wasn't our fault," Orianna said.

"What if these creatures ate the Summer Court?" Derrick asked.

"They are too many other frozen Seelie around, even in the room here," Lockwood said, though his eyes were flitting as he considered the answer. "I cannot imagine they would only eat the court."

"I've always wanted to taste royalty," Iona said. "I imagine there's a fanciness to their blood that others lack."

Aureus blinked, his sword back, ready to attack the moment the ice giants made their move. "...What?"

The ice giants roared and charged, and Lockwood and Orianna struck first, lashing out with their magic. It coruscated across the room...

...and bounced off their icy forms.

"Well, that's not good," Lockwood said, the giants shaking the room as they came for us. It was like standing on the deck of a ship caught in a storm.

"All right, Derrick," I said, waving at him. "Just kind of hang behind me. We're probably gonna run–"

"Don't worry, I got this," he said, pushing past my outstretched arm. His back muscles were taut, hands extended in front of himself as if he thought that he could summon magic of his own.

"Derrick, you don't have to play the hero." I said. "You have the least fighting experience, and I really don't need to get another one of my friends k–"

There was a rustle behind me, and I turned just in time to see Iona leap through the air, leap as if she had some sort of super jump ability. She let out a roar of her own, wound up her fist, pulling it far behind her, before striking out. She crashed into the lead giant with a punch, and it exploded into icy shards. The pieces went flying in every direction, including back toward us.

I leapt aside, Derrick leading me by a few inches, and sharp pieces of the busted giant glittered as it flew past my face. The nearest actually stirred my hair as it whizzed by. Derrick caught me as I started to topple over.

"That would hurt," he said, looking at the wall; the shards were buried in it like bullet holes.

I heard Iona cry out again, and watched as she jumped once more. It was like she had springs in her shoes. She landed on the next giant's back, and it started spinning wildly, trying to grab her off. She was only on it for a second or two, though, before raising her hand and slamming it into the beast's neck.

It shattered like dropped glass, sending pieces flying once more.

This time there was no dodging them all; I felt a sharp pain in my hip, and took a staggering step back. With a cry, I fell to the floor, my teeth gritted with pain.

"Cassie, are you okay?" Derrick said, falling on his knees beside me.

"Don't know," I said, cringing against the pain. My hip burned, and every time I took a deep breath in, there was a sharp sting that sent shivers up my spine.

"Here, let me look at it." Gently, he rolled me over onto my back.

My fingers were trembling and were numb. I could hear the sounds of fighting. Iona let out another crazy battle cry, and I soon heard the sound of more shattering.

Derrick ducked and leaned over me, protecting my lower half which was still exposed to the rest of the room. "It got you, all right," he said, his brow furrowed with concern. "It's not all that big, but you are bleeding.

I lifted my head to look at the wound, and the room spun around me, my stomach roiling and churning like I had eaten day old gas station sushi.

"Lady Cassandra, what has befallen you – oh, heavens, no! A shard?" Aureus knelt beside me opposite Derrick. He took one of my hands in his. I could barely feel his touch my hands were so numb. Iona's face appeared over his shoulder, her brow furrowed with concern.

"You took care of them quick, Iona," Derrick said. "What came over you? I've never seen you fight like that."

She blinked. "I have no idea. It's like...like I suddenly had super powers."

"I mean, you already kind of did," Derrick said. "But the way you leapt at those things...you took them out with one hit."

"Yeah," Iona said, glancing sidelong at Aureus, "it was pretty cool, wasn't it?"

"We need to get Cassandra home," Lockwood said. "There are no answers to be gleaned here. Do you think you can put weight on that leg?" This he said to me.

"I – I think so," I said between deep breaths. "As long as I don't look at it, I think I can deal with it."

"Derrick, help me," Lockwood said. Together, the two of them lifted me as if I weighed nothing, taking care not to jostle the injured hip. I winced as they set me down on my feet, the pain shooting back up my leg.

Derrick swung an arm around my back. "Don't worry, I won't drop you. Lean on me, I've got you."

Grateful that he did indeed seem to have a good grip on me, I tried walking a few feet with him, testing the pain. "It's bad, but I think I can walk."

Iona's eyes peered at my injury. "Is this going to just melt?"

"Unfortunately, no." Lockwood shook his head. "That shard will remain until we are able to extract it."

"Sounds like a job for Dr. Dad," I said. "The sooner, the better."

"You're right, of course," Lockwood said. He gave the room one last, longing look.

"I'm sorry we didn't find anything," I said as sympathetically as I could. The pain was intense.

"At least we aren't leaving entirely empty-handed,"

Orianna said. "We know that the court is not here any longer."

"Indeed," Aureus said with a scowl. "If they have been forced to retreat from Starvale, the fate that has befallen them is perhaps worse than death."

"I will believe nothing until we have seen it for ourselves," Lockwood said. "We must not lose hope. Not now. Not ever."

We made our way toward the doors, leaving with nothing more than a wound in my side – and somehow, even more questions than we came with.

34

Lockwood flew me all the way back to the fountain, slowly, and in silence. The warmth of him helped calm my shivers in the face of the frigid chill. How was Faerie, where this bitter cold was originating, warmer than Tampa had been when we left?

I didn't know. I didn't know anything about anything at this point.

"So..." I said as he landed lightly on the fountain's top tier. "What do we do next, Lockwood?" He set me down gently in the near-freezing water, which sent a shock of numbness across my body, muting the pain from the wound.

I could see by the vacant look in his eyes that he was as lost in this as I was. "I do not know. I had hoped that we would find the answers we needed here. But now that we have nothing, I..." He stared off into space for a few moments, then shook his head, blue hair stirring in the wind.

"What if we went to the Winter Court?" Derrick asked. He'd kept pace with us, surprisingly.

Orianna shook her head. "Our court knows barely anything. In fact, the little I have gleaned since arriving on Earth is far more than I knew when I left."

Derrick nodded his head. "Back at square one, then?"

"Back to Tampa, at least," Lockwood said, then muttered the same words that he had said earlier over the fountain's keystone. The same gripping sensation washed over me. I slammed my eyes shut, not wanting to open them and the pain to overwhelm me. It was pressing in on me, tighter and tighter, when I opened my eyes and we were back on Earth.

"Oh, crap," Iona said, not subtly.

Oh, crap was right.

Everything was covered in white. The grass, the concrete, the asphalt. The sky was still pitch dark overhead, the clouds hanging low in the sky, moving quickly as the chilly wind swirled through the air. The few people out were shuffling through the slush, slipping and sliding as they went. There were marks from where others had slipped recently. The water that spattered against me was bone-chillingly cold, taking my breath away.

"Let's get out of this fountain before anyone sees us," Orianna said.

Under a steady flurrying, Lockwood carried me down the fountain's tiers as I dripped chill water. My teeth were back to chattering, heavier than ever. He fluttered me down to Iona's car with great care, setting me in as I shivered. We all crammed into Iona's car. I fiddled with the seatbelt, trying to make it not land on my wound, which had, at least, stopped bleeding. Any way I tried to position it, I seemed to brush that painful area, bringing welling tears to my eyes.

"Just forget the seat belt," Iona said. "My boyfriend can grab you if I hit the brakes too fast."

I looked back at Aureus, who was staring at me with

wide eyes. Still, he managed to say, "Of course. I shall protect you from this mighty beast with my very life, should it rear and try to throw us."

"I love how he puts his whole heart into everything," Iona said. If she could have, she would have sighed.

My head sagged back against the headrest, and I closed my eyes.

The pain was so bad that I was fighting the battle to stay conscious again. My limbs felt like lead, and even sitting there perfectly still while Iona struggled to get the engine to turn over in the cold was not enough. Soon I felt the car moving underneath me, but I just wanted to give into the darkness, to the quiet.

My mind drifted, muffled by the pain in my hip. I thought of Xandra, a nightmarish vision of her launching from beneath her bed, fangs bared, ready to bite me…maybe in that sharp, painful place in my hip…

Xandra. Where was she? What was she doing? Was she okay? If she was okay, did that mean that other people had gotten hurt? The idea of seeing her sinking her teeth into another person just like Mill had was too much for my addled brain to handle.

If she was feeding, though, we were racing to a familiar ending…which was sinking my stake into her heart.

The idea curdled my stomach. I couldn't imagine staring into her face, my best friend's face, and forcing my hand to do what I didn't ever think I'd be able to.

The car thumped to a stop and I jolted awake. Snow had piled at the edges of the windows, and it took me a moment to realize I was staring out at my lawn, my house, blanketed in a thick layer of white. Derrick had opened the passenger door, and the lights inside the car flared to life, making me blink against the spell of what I was seeing. Strange magic.

When he lifted me out of the warm seat and into the freezing air, pain shot down my side, and I cringed, letting out a little moan. I felt groggy as he carried me across the snowswept yard toward the front door.

"I called your mother on the way home," Lockwood said, pacing us. "Your father is on his way home."

"That's not good. I don't want him to worry," I said as Derrick carried me smoothly along. "You're strong."

He gave me a goofy sort of grin. "Uh...thanks."

"Are you working out now or something?" I said.

"Not exactly, no," he said.

"Come on, everybody," I said, with a sleepy, dreamlike quality to my words, "let's get inside."

Aureus was holding the front door open, and the dramatic temperature change coming in out of the flurrying was fantastic, the chill suddenly reducing just a tinge. "I shall accompany you inside," Aureus announced. "And protect the castle from within." He hesitated. "For it is far too cold for a servant of Summer be outside."

"Cassie, is that you?" I heard Mom call from the kitchen.

"Yeah, Mom," I said as Derrick carried me in her direction. "Is Dad home yet?"

"No, he's not." Her voice carried around the corner. "He's stuck at the hospital. Apparently these damn Yankees who have moved down here forgot how to drive in the snow. Or maybe the native Floridians never did." She came around the corner, took one look at me, and dropped her coffee mug. It splattered at her feet. With her jaw hanging for a moment, she took me in, then whispered, "I didn't realize it was that bad."

"I'm fine, Mom, it's not a big deal," I said. It occurred to me I'd just lied, so I hurriedly called it out. "Okay, no, it is actually a big deal. I can't walk like this."

She hurried over. "What is this thing sticking out of your hip?"

"It's...hard to explain," I said.

"It's a shard of a giant monster Iona punched to pieces," Derrick said, still holding me effortlessly.

My mother gave him a look. "I liked her lack of explanation better."

She helped Derrick move me to the couch, where the towels laid out for Iona still waited. I winced as the shard sent a twinge of pain down my leg. Mom knelt down beside me, examining the wound.

"Honey, if your dad was here, he would be able to check it out for you, but there isn't really anything that I can do," she said. There were bags under her eyes, which were bloodshot and watery. "Other than prepare a lawsuit, which...I'm not sure who to even send it to."

"Probably the Seelie Court of Faerie," I said, "since I was on their property at the time."

"We don't really wear suits there," Aureus announced, still brushing the snow out of his golden locks. "Though I am sure whatever type of cloth your 'law' is, it would be exceptional."

"It's mostly paper these days," I said dryly. "I think maybe I'll just lie here for a bit." The cold had a narcotic quality to it, my clothing felt frozen to my skin. Numbness was like a blanket keeping out the worst of the pain, that sharp stabbing at my hip when I moved it, or breathed wrong a not-so-gentle reminder of my wound.

"We don't need you falling asleep if you're hypothermic and losing blood," Derrick said. "You need to stay awake, and we need to warm her up."

"I could look at it," Orianna said, fluttering over the couch to kneel beside me. "I know that we didn't discuss it when we were in Faerie, but we have magic that could seal that wound."

"Absolutely not," Lockwood said, with a surprising fire in his eyes. "Faerie healing magic is untested on humans. I would not dare try it unless the situation were dire."

"Well, why not now?" Orianna protested. "She needs help, doesn't she?"

"Do you have any idea how awry Fae magic can go here?" Lockwood asked. "No, you don't, because you've just arrived. I have been here, and I have seen the horrors that can be unleashed by casual use of seemingly-mundane spells go terribly, awfully wrong."

"What...what happened?" Derrick asked, looking from Orianna to Lockwood. "Did somebody die?"

"Nothing so dramatic as that," Lockwood huffed. When he noticed the press of all of our eyes on him, he seemed to blush. "I am perhaps overstating it. Still – Fae magic does not always work as intended in this realm. It is not a cure-all."

"I'm really wondering what he did now," Iona said with a hint of a sly grin. "Did you try to glamour one of your fancy cars and turn it into a stallion?"

"I – no!" Lockwood said with a bit too much starch in his denial. His face fell a moment later. "Well – yes. When I first arrived, I did attempt to 'break into' the chauffeur game by turning an old Honda Civic into a stretch. It ended – shall we say – poorly."

Derrick was trying to conceal his smile. Trying, and failing. "What, uh...what happened there?"

"I lost a rather sizable contract," Lockwood said stiffly, "and a certain starlet in town to shoot a movie lost a dress, her shoes, and – well, more." He reddened. "Quite a bit more, in fact." And he looked away. "In my defense, she did not lose anything that was authentically hers. Just, the, uhm...artificial...parts added by a team of skilled surgeons, I'm sure–"

Iona cackled, and it set the rest of us off. Even me, though...boy, did it hurt.

"So can you fix this?" My mother asked Orianna. "Without accidentally turning her bones into porridge or something?"

"All I will say is that silicon is not meant to be in the body," Lockwood said. "If we could just hew to simple principles such as that – not in the chest, nor in the bottom–"

"I definitely don't have any of that," I said, grimacing as I touched the painful wound at my hip. "This is the only artificial thing in me so far as I know."

"It's absolutely possible to heal this," Orianna said.

"You don't know that," Lockwood said, "and you won't know it until you've succeeded – here, get out of the way." And he practically pushed her aside. "If anyone is to attempt this, it should be someone with knowledge of magic use here."

"Thank you, Lockwood," I said, feeling weak, the chill long-since settled on my bones like an ache.

He looked me in the eyes, and his were rimmed with concern. "The only way that we are going to be able to do this is to extract the shard by magic and then magically cauterize the wound."

I sighed, my heart starting to beat faster. "This is going to hurt a lot, isn't it?"

Lockwood looked at me with pity. "To dull the pain would require powerful magic, a sleeping spell or something of that sort. I wouldn't dare it unless there were no other option, for fear you might not wake up for days...if ever."

"I guess I'll take the pain," I said. "No real time to sleep just now.

"Here," Mom said, reappearing behind the couch with a washcloth in her hands that was rolled up like a burrito. "If there's going to be pain, you might want to bite down on this instead of your own tongue."

Cold fear swept over me as I looked at Lockwood. He nodded. "That seems wise."

I lay my head back against the couch, aware of how much it smelled like Mom's favorite candles and the laundry detergent, since she always folded the towels and blankets here on the couch. I clamped the washcloth between my teeth, my gag reflex already threatening to react from the feeling of the scratchy cloth on my tongue.

I nodded to Lockwood that I was ready. My heart was in my throat and my stomach in knots as I squeezed my eyes shut tight, biting down on the cloth as hard as I could. Pain radiated out from the wound as Lockwood touched the shard.

"It's not very deep, thankfully," he said. "All right, Cassandra, on the count of three. One – two –"

And then he yanked.

The shard sprung free, leaving an icy ache behind. Other than the spear of discomfort when he'd pulled it, it didn't feel too bad, and I said so.

"Good. Now bite down. I am going to cauterize it," he said.

There was a sudden flare of heat and a glow against my eyelids. It was as if Lockwood was holding a blow torch.

I arched my back, trying desperately to move as far from the pain as I could. I was glad that I had the washcloth in my mouth, because not only did it prevent me from biting off my own tongue, but it helped muffle the scream that came barreling out of me in response.

It was blinding, white hot, and made me certain it was going to burn me alive. I had seared my hands on pots and pans before, even on my hair straightener when I bothered to use the stupid thing. But this...this was a completely different level of pain. It was so hot it was almost cold, like a knife being shoved into my side.

Mom was there, stroking my forehead which was now beaded with sweat. I was gasping for breath, the washcloth having absorbed all of the moisture in my mouth.

"It's okay, Cassandra, it's all right," Lockwood was saying from somewhere far away. "It's done."

I opened my eyes and forced myself to focus. Lockwood had sealed the wound completely shut. It was black and charred, like he had placed a lump of charcoal on my side, but it wasn't any bigger than a dime.

"Are you all right, dear?" Mom asked. She was still stroking my hair, trying hard to hide the concern in her face.

"I think so," I said, voice croaking once I removed the washcloth. The exhaustion was tenfold now, and I felt like I was going to pass out. "Mom, could you brew me a pot of coffee? I need it."

"Sure, sweetie," Mom said. No argument about the dangers of caffeine. Yay.

"I need to see if I can walk," I said. "Can someone help me up?"

Lockwood stooped and wrapped his arm around me, hoisting me onto my feet. Once there, he allowed me to test my weight on that leg.

It held, shockingly. The knots in my stomach loosened as I smiled back at Lockwood. "Thank you. I don't know what you did exactly, and I'm not positive I really want to, but whatever it was, it worked."

He nodded his head. "My pleasure, Lady Cassandra, and the least I could do given your sacrifice trying to help my homeland." I started to move away and he seized my arm. "What are you doing?"

"I need a hot shower and a change of clothes," I said. "Every part of me except that which you just burned is frigging freezing." I ran a hand through my hair; little pieces of snow were still stuck in it.

"You sure that you'll be able to make it up the stairs?" Mom called from the kitchen, already hard at work on my coffee.

I hobbled across the living room. "Yeah, I'll be fine. Besides, I don't have time to be sitting here on my butt while the whole world is turning into a winter wonderland. Just a quick refresh and I'll be back for that coffee." I felt like I was dragging. Hopefully the warmth of the shower would revive me.

I turned and made my way up the stairs, testing the wound. It was tender and there was still an ache around the area Lockwood had burned, but it wasn't nearly as bad as it was when the shard was still buried there. The one good thing about the steady, radiating pain is that it woke me up. As long as I didn't sit down and remember how exhausted I was, the constant, spearing pain would probably keep me conscious.

I ducked into my room, which was dark and chilly, a bit like walking into a freezer. I wrapped my arms around myself, shucking off Derrick's wet sweatshirt onto the floor. My breath hung in the air as I surveyed the room; a slight breeze was coming from the window, which was open a crack. Snow coated the sill, and a line of it dusted the carpet below.

"Sonofa," I muttered. Stupid. Leaving the window open in Florida on a summer night? Not a great idea if only because it rained pretty regularly here. I hobbled my way to the window and slammed it shut. I'd have to deal with the snow pile, too, because Mom would flip if she found a giant mildew spot in the new carpet.

Staring at the snow, I realized...there were a couple small, partially snowed over indentations there, like someone – or something – had left their footprints. They were mostly covered over now, but still, they were there, two small footprints.

I held my breath for a few seconds, listening hard.

There was no breath on the back of my neck, but I could feel someone standing there.

I was just opening my mouth to shout for someone, anyone, when a hand as cold as death closed over my mouth, preventing me from getting the scream out. I was pressed against someone so hard it was like I was gripped by metal made freezing cold by the winter weather.

I craned my neck to see who it belonged to, my heart hammering against my ribs–

And no heart beat at all in the chest I was snugged tight against. Cold, dark eyes glared down at me, clamping my mouth shut with a dead hand so no sound could escape.

It was Xandra.

She had me.

35

Xandra was here, in my bedroom, just like she always used to be. But now it was cold, and dark, and there were no chick flicks playing in the background, and no sharp tang of nail polish as we painted our toes bright obnoxious colors. No sleepy conversations, making plans for the weekend, and there was definitely not any laughter.

Her hands were so cold. Cold like death, cold like she'd been out in the winter all night long.

Of course...she had been.

But how did she get in? She was a vampire now, she couldn't have gotten in unless I invited–

My skin crawled as I realized that she must have taken my flippant, half-unconscious suggestion to the others that we get inside as a red-carpet invitation to come on in. Through my bedroom window, no less.

My breathing was coming in quick, sharp bursts. Her hand was cupped over my mouth, but she had left my nose free. My head swam as I caught the faintest trace of her perfume. My heart ached. This wasn't like being pinned by just any vampire.

This was Xandra. Like Jacquelyn all over again.

In this situation, it was going to have to be either her or me. And it couldn't be me, not when my mom was downstairs. Lockwood, Iona, and the other two Fae might be able to deal with her before she caused too much damage, but what would happen when they came up here and realized what she'd done to me? I imagined myself drained of blood, pale, sprawled on the carpet with twin dribblings of red down my neck.

I tried to shake her off, but her grip was cold steel. I had to put distance between us. I needed to get to the stake in my hair. And if I couldn't reach that, then I had spares over on my dresser. If I could duck out from under her grip, I might be able to make it to the bed in time to pull a stake, ready myself, and place it between her ribs when she leapt for me like a hungry, angry jungle cat.

The idea sickened me, and my head swam. I couldn't kill Xandra–

But I had to.

I pushed out with my hip to knock her off balance, and it screamed pain. I tried to ignore it, marshaling myself to duck out from underneath her hand. She started to fall forward at the same time that I spun on my feet, sliding the stake out of my hair.

But she was quick, and as if she knew what I was doing, she knocked the stake out of my hand, stretching my arm out far to my side, keeping it away from herself. It clattered against the far wall, making a terrible noise. She grabbed the front of my shirt and yanked me toward her. I wavered, and she was able to shove me to the ground.

She pinned me to the damp carpet, her hand flat on my sternum. She was so strong that the pressure alone made it hard for me to breathe. I sputtered and coughed, trying to pry her hand from my chest, and braced for the impact that I knew was coming–

"Cassie."

Cold pressure rested on me, more than just her weight. The stake was against my fingertips, flat on the carpet, just at the edge of my reach. I brushed my fingers against it, trying to roll it toward me, to get it in my hand...

"Cassie...it's me," she whispered.

I opened my eyes, staring up at her. The face that I saw was not one of anger, hate, or even cold, hungry malice.

Her icy blue eyes were wide, sad. Desperate. Afraid.

My hands shook, fingertips resting on the wood stake as I stared up at her. "Xan...Xandra?" I said, my voice cracking. I couldn't let myself believe it. She – she was gone. This couldn't be. It couldn't–

"It's me," she whispered, cold as death and not breathing.

She lifted her hand away from my collarbone and sat back, resting her hands on her knees. The movement was very fluid, like a cat.

"Xandra?" I asked again. Like I would get a different answer. I sat up slowly, massaging the sore spot on my chest. I'd probably have a bruise there later. I just stared at her, my heart beating rapidly. I wanted to believe it, wanted so badly to believe it was her.

She tilted her head to the side slightly, hair falling over her shoulder. Something about the movement seemed so natural, so familiar that my heart lurched in my chest. I had seen her do it a thousand times. "It's me." Her voice sounded rough. "I'm a vampire but...somehow...I'm still *me.*"

"But you were dead," I whispered. I touched her hand, felt her wrist – so cold, and no pulse. "I thought you were – thought you were becoming..."

"I'm sorry I scared you," Xandra said. "The hunger, the urge, it's...intense."

"Why are you apologizing to me?" I said, pulling my hand away. "You have nothing to apologize about. It was my fault that this happened to you–"

"Cassie," Xandra said. "It's not your fault. Why do you always blame yourself for everything that happens?"

"Because it is my fault, this *is* my fault." I stared into her eyes. "If not for me, you'd be alive right now–"

"You don't know that," Xandra said, shaking her head. "Maybe Byron would have latched onto me if you hadn't been here. I was walking home that night, remember?" She stared down at her hands. "Maybe this was always my destiny."

"It really is you," I said softly.

"It really is," she said, and reached out a hand. I took it, and in spite of the cold fingers, I knew...

Somehow...I had my best friend back.

36

"We need to tell everyone," I said after two minutes of hugging, of gabbing, of my tiredness suddenly erased like I'd had a long nap. For these glorious moments, I'd been aware of only Xandra, of the fact that my best friend had, for all intents and purposes, come back from the dead.

It was hard to forget, though, the world was sort of falling apart around me, and it wasn't until Xandra asked me why I'd been wearing a guy's sweatshirt that was totally not in Mill's style, that I recalled all the things my tired mind had let go in the excitement of her return.

"Who is everyone, exactly?" she asked, pale face screwed up genuine curiosity.

"Come on," I said, staggering to my feet. The burnt spot on my hip ached and throbbed. I grabbed it, massaging the charred flesh.

"Also, I was going to ask but didn't want you to think that I was about to eat you...why do you smell like you've been bled and partially cooked?" She made a vague gesture toward my wound.

I flushed, realizing that I was covered in blood in front of a new vampire. "I'll explain later. Come on, let's go down-stairs." I paused. "Better let me lead."

"Hey, guys," I announced as I was getting close to the bottom of the stairs, "good news. I found Xandra, and she's actually not evil."

I hit the bottom stair with Xandra directly behind me only to find everyone in the room readying themselves for a fight. Orianna, Aureus, and Lockwood had magic glowing from their hands, Derrick was like a UFC fighter, his hands balled into fists, his jaw clenched, and his back strangely arched. Iona...I didn't even see her.

Mom was staring at Xandra like she had seen a ghost. I knew the feeling.

"Whoa, be cool, people, be cool," I said, holding my hands up.

Xandra was peering around me with wide eyes that reminded me a lot of Orianna. "Wow. Full house."

"She's fine," I said, still holding my hands up in surren-der. The last thing that we needed was to piss off an entire room filled of powerful creatures. "For real fine."

"I did not see this beautiful creature enter the house," Aureus said, brandishing his glowing sword. "Lady Cassan-dra, I have failed you." And then he took a knee.

"Beautiful creature?" Xandra said. Then she giggled, very on point for her.

"Back off, anime kitty," Iona spat, her eyes flashing. She'd appeared at the side of the stairs, apparently hiding in their shadow. Now she was only a couple feet from Xandra, ready to engage.

"Calm, Iona," I said, positioned myself between them. "She's fine."

Iona's amber eyes flashed, and I saw a hint of the monster within. "Vampires are generally not 'fine.'"

"Are you?" I asked. She had her teeth bared, fangs out, and they seemed to recede as I watched.

Xandra shrugged. "I didn't think I'd be welcome if I just showed up at the door. So I came in the upstairs window."

Iona's eyes slowly closed, pained. "I have warned her about being overly inviting."

"Yeah, that's something she really needs to watch," Xandra said, looking right at me. "What if Varycas and Jac-a-whacka-whacka had been hiding in the bushes instead of me? It would have been a wipeout."

"Did you just call her Jac-a-whacka-whacka?" I asked, giving Xandra a most-perturbed look.

"Cassandra, I–" Mom started. Her hand was over her heart, her eyes wide as she started between Xandra and me. "How did she – why is she–"

"Okay, yes, this is a lot to take in," I said. There was still a little chill in the air, and my clothes were clinging wet and cold to me, but fortunately it was a touch warmer down here.

Iona was trying to glare at Xandra around me. "Why are you so quick to buy that she's fully herself again?"

"Well, for one, she cornered me in my room and didn't eat me," I said. "Vampires that don't eat me get points."

"I got points." Xandra nodded her head.

"This is the girl that we chased to that Lord of Edutation's lands tonight?" Orianna asked.

"Is she wearing your favorite outfit?" Xandra asked. If I needed more proof she was back, she looked offended on my behalf.

"Yeah," I said. "We'll talk about that later."

"I, for one, am so pleased to see you returned to us, Lady Alexandra," Lockwood said with a deep bow. "You have no idea the despair that your absence has caused us. Truly, this long night that has fallen seemed perfectly matched to the hour of your funeral rites."

"Wow, Lockwood," Xandra said. "Thanks. That's super nice."

"It's crazy," I said. "I guess she came out the other side of her blood madness...or whatever."

Derrick grinned, relaxing his stance. "Just gonna say, 'Blood madness' is an awesome name for a video game."

"Right?" Xandra agreed. "Like a sweet Mortal Kombat expansion. Ooh, or maybe a horror visual novel."

Iona's gaze hardened, if that was possible. "Prove that it's you. That you're in your right mind."

Xandra smirked, popping out her hip. "Stand down, Elsa."

"It's thematically correct." Iona eased up a little, folding her arms over her chest. "All right, fine, she's got her brain back about her."

Xandra grinned.

"Does she – " Mom started, looking at me. Then her gaze shifted to Xandra. "What about your parents? They need to know that you're okay – "

"One crisis at a time, please," I said. "For now, we have to deal with the fact that Siberia has come to Florida."

Mom glanced out of the window in the kitchen, her face falling. Like the snow outside.

"Yeah, that's pretty much why I came," Xandra said. "I'm assuming that you're at the center of it again?"

"Good assumption," I said.

"Well, count me in." She grinned. "I'm on Team Epic. But with teeth this time. And claws. Rawr." Her eyes narrowed and darted toward the other side of the room. She pointed a finger in Aureus's direction. "But I don't think he is."

My heart jolted. "But what do you me—"

He moved as fast as lightning. One second Aureus was standing near Lockwood and Orianna, the next he was across the room and yanking Iona off her feet, grabbing her around the neck, pulling her tight to him.

She giggled at his wrist around her neck. "I don't breathe, you know. And I don't go really go for the rough stu—"

Aureus's aloof expression was gone, replaced with a hard, dark look. There was a flash, and his glowing sword was pointed right at the small of her back.

"Oh," Iona said, "well...that could be a problem."

37

"Whoa, easy, Aureus," I said, holding my hands up. War about to break out in my living room. Again. "What are you doing?"

Aureus was glaring at us all, his sword still pointed at Iona's back.

"Seriously, sweetheart," Iona said. "this isn't funny."

"I am disgusted that a demonic evil like this creature was brought into the magical lands of Summer," Aureus said. "That I held her in my holy arms is an affront to righteousness."

"Hey, you let Gladys touch you, okay?" Iona said, looking righteously affronted herself. "I can still smell the old lady scent on you, I don't think I'm the problem."

"Aureus, what are you doing?" Lockwood asked, edging to the side. We were slowly trying to flank him, to surround him. "Iona is not our enemy."

"It's not her that concerns me," Aureus said, "though you should be ashamed to associate with creatures of the darkness like this, Paladin."

Lockwood wilted slightly. "What are you talking about?"

Aureus turned and looked at me. "Lady Cassandra, I am sorry that I used you, but it was necessary to obtain the information that I needed. You are just as resourceful and as formidable as I was told you were."

"What information did you need?" I said, eyeing the sword at Iona's back.

"I needed to know the truth about what Winter knows," he said, shooting a sidelong look in Orianna's direction.

"Which is nothing more than you do," Orianna said.

Aureus looked around at us all. "I've been sent by the King of Summer. He knew that Winter would send its representatives here, sneaking around, while they prepared a first strike against us."

"Winter is not trying to war against you." Orianna fluttered a couple feet off the floor, hair swirling around her angrily. "We had nothing to do with whatever has happened to your court. Whoever did this to Summer, made them relinquish their responsibilities, it wasn't us–"

"The King of Summer has not relinquished responsibilities," Aureus said. "He is firmly in control."

"The king?" I asked. "Okay, but what about the queen? What happened to her?"

Aureus seemed uncomfortable with that question. "She was...deposed, just as you heard."

"You've been here for weeks." My eyes narrowed. "Did you know that she was going to be deposed?"

"Hello, prisoner here," Iona said. "If I still got aches, I'd definitely have a serious one right about now." She was standing at a strange angle, trying to prevent his sword point from making contact with her back. "Can we resolve this?"

"It was a possibility with the king's plans–" Aureus began.

"One moment," Lockwood said, a hard expression on his face. "Is the king attempting to sit on the throne?"

"He is, yes," Aureus said, his chest puffing up, his gaze sharpening. "After the dismal failures of the past, Summer requires a new leader. Someone with strength to guide us out of this period of humiliation and decline."

"But the power sits with the queen, just as it always has," Orianna said, her mouth slightly open in horror.

"There is no possible way that the king can take up the mantle," Lockwood said.

"What does that mean?" I asked. "The king can't sit on the throne?"

"He cannot take up the power of the seat, no," Lockwood said. "This explains so much...if the king has something to do with the queen's fall–"

"He is going to succeed where no other has before," Aureus said in a boisterous tone. "We are going to win, and claim all of Faerie in the name of Summer. Never again will we suffer the humiliation–"

Iona gave me a short nod, and I realized that she had been sand bagging the whole time, not wanting to stop Aureus before he gave up all he knew.

I laughed, then glanced pointedly out the window. Big, fat flakes were falling outside as if we were staring into a life size snow globe. "It's snowing in summer. Isn't that a little humiliating?"

"Laugh all you want," Aureus said, "but the king has discovered a way to keep the throne."

Lockwood's face paled and he took a step toward Aureus. "How? How exactly does he plan to pervert the natural order of power?"

"He has found a way to transfer the power to himself," Aureus said. "You will see."

Even Orianna's face lost some color. "That is not how Faerie works."

"That's not how any of this works," Xandra said, drawing every eye in the room. "You cannot start that meme and not expect me to complete it."

"How is the king to do this?" Lockwood asked.

Aureus threw his head back and laughed. "I am but the humble Knight who serves the crown. The ways of the Court are beyond us, Paladin."

"So you don't know." Iona gave me another annoyed look. "Do we have everything we need?"

I folded my arms. "I think this just about covers it unless you have something to add?"

"No," Aureus said. "I have nothing left to add now that you know there is nothing that you can do to stop us. Our power will be complete. Our reign, unstoppable—"

"Oh, really?" Iona stopped slumping like a ragdoll and heaved him up and over herself. He crashed out the window behind her, as if he weighed nothing at all. He couldn't even stop himself, she chucked him so hard.

After a moment he popped back up from his hard landing, covered in fine, powdery snow. Scrapes oozed silvery blood from his arms and face and he swayed, disoriented. "All right, but that did not stop me!" he said, and then fluttered off into the night. "I am not stopped!" His voice trailed off under the noise-dampening fall of snow.

"We just gonna let him go?" Xandra said. "Just let him run off cackling into the night? After that monologue?"

"Somehow, I doubt he has more information," Lockwood said. "I have never heard of such a thing, taking power from the queen. It's not possible...or at least I did not think it was."

"I'm no expert," I said, peering out the window, "but it's not looking possible. It's looking like an epic fail."

Orianna flittered behind me, peering out into the artificial night. "I shudder to say...but I agree with Lockwood."

"Now I am even more uncertain," Lockwood muttered.

I looked over at Iona. "You can track him in this, right?"

Xandra stepped in front of me, grinning. "If she can't, I can. I can smell that old lady perfume a mile off."

"It should have been my perfume," Iona said, so quietly I wondered if she realized she'd said it aloud.

"Great, we give him a little lead," I said, "then we run him down to wherever he's going."

Mom wandered over to stand beside Orianna, also staring out of the window. "Cassandra, I appreciate that your friends want to help, but...couldn't we have tossed the sword flailing faerie out the front door?" Her grimace was pained. "The home repairs are really starting to mount up, dear. Plus, it's a little drafty in here now–"

As I stood there, looking at the broken window, the surviving glass began to frost over. It reached out, forming a new impermeable membrane of crystal ice, filling the gaps and covering the window over entirely.

"That's a little weird, right?" Xandra asked. "The window repairing itself with ice? Or is it just that cold now?"

Orianna dropped to a knee, bowing her head.

"And now it looks like a Major League Soccer game is about to begin," Xandra said.

Lockwood had stiffened, his back straight, shoulders tense. "Someone...is here."

"A whole room full of them, in fact," my mom muttered. But before she finished, I heard a soft knock at the door. Xandra and Iona moved to flank me, as if acting as my protectors. Derrick did too...which was strange.

"Evil doesn't usually knock, does it?" I asked, moving past them. "It's more of a doorbell thing, right?" No one stopped me, so I pulled open the door.

And my jaw hit the floor.

"She should be Elsa, not me," Iona muttered.

A beautiful woman in a pearly white dress with wings like silvery mist, and voluminous, raven black curls waited on my stoop. Her lips curled up one side of her face in a smirk. Ice followed after her, perfect crystalized footsteps leading up the front path to where she stood.

"You're not wrong," I said. "Because unless my memory fails...this is Pruina." When that revelation produced dead silence, I added, "The Winter Queen herself."

"Your Majesty," Orianna said with a voice tinged with awe. I didn't miss my guess.

Winter was here.

38

"Um...welcome, Your Majesty," I said, inclining my head to her as I stood holding my door open to the Faerie Queen of Winter. The bite in the air was even stronger, like the worst snowstorm that I could remember. The little hairs inside my nose were starting to freeze. I was still in Tampa, right?

"Cassandra, isn't it?" the queen said, arching a perfect eyebrow at me.

"Yeah," I said, looking back up at her. "I mean, yes." Formal felt right, in spite of my tattered, unshowered appearance.

"Cassandra, who is this?" Mom said. Her eyes widened as they fell on the Winter Queen. "Oh." It didn't take me repeating myself to make her realize that this was royalty on our doorstep.

"May I come in?" the queen asked. Because I'd forgotten my manners.

Xandra just shook her head. "Invite in any random vamp or fae, but leave an *actual queen* standing on the doorstep until she invites herself in."

"Please, come in," I said, waving her toward the kitchen. "Can I, uh, get you something to drink? Coffee? Tea?" I threw an emergency look at Lockwood. "What do they eat in Faerie?"

Lockwood just shrugged. He looked dumbstruck, or as close to it as I'd ever seen him.

The queen stepped in as gracefully as I remembered, long dress trailing behind her. Little flakes of snow seemed to follow, disappearing just before they struck the floor. "Nothing, thank you. Unfortunately, this is not a social call." She looked over at Orianna, who was still kneeling. "My loyal servant...rise."

Orianna jumped up, and I watched as her glamour faded away. Her golden wings fluttered and she was practically gawking at the queen.

The queen then took us all in with a careful, slow-moving gaze. She nodded at each in turn, until she reached Derrick, at which point she arched a brow, her nostrils flaring. That was weird.

"The Seelie Knight." Her icy blue eyes fell upon Lockwood, and she stood straighter. "I see that you are still in service to the humans."

Lockwood's gaze hardened, and he folded his arms across his chest, giving her a cool look.

"I am not condemning you," the queen said easily, her face remaining calm and collected. She folded her hands in front of herself. "In fact...I must ask you both for your help once again."

Lockwood's face softened ever so slightly. "What could we do that you could not? It doesn't seem as if Winter's powers are lacking."

"Power is not at issue." The queen looked at him unflinchingly. "I cannot intervene in this matter."

"Wait, what?" Iona asked.

"That doesn't make sense," Xandra said.

"You can't do *anything*?" I said.

"It is very simple, really," said the queen. She looked at Lockwood. "This matter concerns the Seelie Court. The king is attempting to try and transfer the Summer Queen's essence of power, her mantle, to himself."

"What does that mean?" I said.

The queen nodded. "Part of the Seelie and Unseelie Courts' job is to maintain balance in Faerie, but also to protect the wards between our world and Earth. Since part of the power has been removed, the wards that make a border between our worlds have weakened, and Unseelie magic has been spilling over without opposition."

"That all makes sense," I said, "but what do you want us to do about it? I mean, what *can* we even do?"

"The transfer of power is going to be happening here, on Earth," the queen said.

Lockwood's jaw dropped. "What?"

"At least they are going to attempt it," said the queen. "Where the veil between the worlds is thinnest. The queen has been here on Earth for some while as they prepare, which is why she wasn't at the court when you visited."

"Of course they decided to do it in Tampa." I sighed. "Why does everything fall to us?"

"Unfortunately," she said, "this turn of events affects not only Faerie, but also your city. If the Summer Queen perishes, as she most likely will when the king attempts to take the power from her, that power will be unleashed – and this place will end up a smoking crater."

Lockwood's face had tightened, and he nodded. "Like a magical nuclear bomb."

"The king is not going to be able to handle the power he

is trying to take," the queen said. "He lacks the skill, the control, the discipline, and – frankly – the wit to know any of this." She drew herself up. "You are the only one who can stop him. I am not allowed to intervene in the affairs of Summer, and there is no one else capable or available. You are the only one who can save your world...save all of us from ruin."

"Yay." I swallowed nervously, the knot in my chest tightening. "I'm special."

"You are, Cassie." Xandra was staring at me with an unmistakable lack of irony.

"I agree with this sentiment, Lady Cassandra," Lockwood said. "You have proven you are capable of handling mystical troubles. And we will be right there with you, helping you every step of the way."

I looked around the room to find all the faces that were looking back at me, expectant.

"When did I get turned into, like, the Knight of Tampa?" I asked. "Why do I get saddled with protecting it from all these threats – the vamps, the fae, the werewolves..."

"Yeah, werewolves." Derrick cleared his throat. "Super dangerous. Totally dangerous."

I sighed. "I don't have a choice, do I?"

"You always had a choice, Cassie," my mother said sadly, from the edge of the kitchen. "You just weren't always exceptionally good at looking down the road and seeing where that choice would lead you." She crossed over to me, taking up my hand. "It's why you lied for so long. But what you didn't realize – what I don't think any of us realized – is that somewhere along the way...you figured it out, sweetie. You know now what will happen if you don't deal with this."

"Tampa go boom," I said sadly, feeling the warmth of her hand on mine. "And Earth enters a new ice age." I could see the begrudging acknowledgment there on her face. Here I was, her daughter, about to go and save Tampa, *again*, and the world from the next ice age.

"It's still your choice," she said. "Just now...you're accepting responsibility for what happens after."

Was she right? She felt right, and that kind of bothered me. "Okay," I said, squaring my shoulders. "Let's do this."

Winter had gone on long enough.

39

Since I was the only one in the whole group who actually knew anything about driving in the snow, I both offered and had no choice but to be the designated driver to our destination. I didn't tell them that I really only had one winter of driving under my belt, since I had gotten my license only about a year before moving down here.

Still, Lockwood had managed to secure a really nice SUV for us. He really liked his Mercedes, didn't he? It was equipped with all-weather tires, which weren't as good as snow tires since the roads were definitely not going to be salted, at least I had some hope of keeping some grip on the road. I wished that I could have asked my dad about the finer points of driving in heavy snow, but figured he might freak out a little if I told him I were going out in this weather in the first place. Especially given his emergency room was currently inundated with injuries from car accidents caused by...driving in the snow.

"I know it's kind of scary," Derrick said, looking out the passenger side window, "but it's also kinda pretty." Our resident fae were flying overhead, and Iona and Xandra were running alongside the car, easily keeping the (slow) pace.

"Derrick," I said, giving him a searching look, "are you really sure you want to do this? I mean, Laura and Gregory aren't here to help this time."

"No, Gregory's probably hiding under his blankets in his room using the excuse to play video games," Derrick said, snorting with laughter. He paused, soberly. "You know they would have come to help if you had called and told them what was happening."

My grip tightened on the wheel. "I am not dragging anyone else into this that I don't have to." I caught a glimpse of Xandra in the headlights, pale and moving at an inhuman pace. I found it hard not to shudder.

I slowed the car. Iona's silvery blonde hair was blowing in the direction that she was looking, across her face. She turned her amber eyes to me and nodded. I couldn't see a damned thing; I was snowblind and had to trust the vampire knew what she was doing. Or sniffing, at least. "I think we're here."

Stepping out into the downrushing snow, I caught sight of a sign that read "Kiley Garden."

"I know this place," Derrick said, catching flakes in his blond hair. "It's a park, right on the Hillsborough River. It's really cool, because it looks like a giant chessboard made from grass and concrete squares." He peered into the utter dark. "Though you can't see that in the snow."

I sighed, steeling myself. A low burn started in my chest. Another fight. Another day.

I wondered if my life as a normal teenager was actually just a dream, one that I had finally awakened from...because this felt like my life now. Friends who were vampires. Fae. I glanced at Derrick – or possibly just nuts.

"All right," I said, the snow coming down wildly around me. "Let's do this."

40

"Not gonna lie, Cassie. Those are pretty sick," Derrick said, glancing down at my hands as we walked through the accumulating snow.

I grinned, flexing my fingers. "Yeah, not too bad for a few nails and a hammer, huh? Glad Dad had a few lying around." I was gripping a narrow piece of wood that I had knocked three nails through. When I wrapped my hands around it, the nails stuck between my fingers like a cat's claws. One nail had seemed to work well at Coldsnap, so why not take it up a notch? "You sure you don't want a pair?"

He shook his head. "I don't need it."

My eyes narrowed. "I don't see–"

"Hey, Cassie," Iona called from ahead, in the snow. "We're about to have company."

I turned and looked over my shoulder. It was hard to see through the snow, but I could just make out an enormous, cylindrical building off to the left, climbing high into the sky. I knew the river was somewhere ahead of me. Iona stood at the top of very short set of stairs. She was staring out over the flat, snow-covered park, her hands balled into fists.

The air was incredibly cold here, and I was having a hard time keeping myself from shivering. I had managed to suit up in my old skiing gear. I even had a few hand warmers left in the pockets that were now radiating their chemical heat in my gloves. I would have preferred the pair of running leggings that I got from UniQlo and a dry-fit top, but I would have frozen to death in those.

Reaching the short steps where Iona waited, I could see the whole park. With all the snow and darkness, lamplights were only my guide to where the river lay, a pitch black mass where the lamps just ended. At the far end of the park, I could see a swirling light, like colored forks of lightning, partially hidden by a wall.

"That's the amphitheater," Derrick said, his blond hair swirling.

That wasn't all that had my attention, though. There was a line of golden-armored soldiers walking toward us out of the swirling snow. They even had helmets on that covered their faces, and were adorned with brightly colored feathers.

"Paladins," Lockwood said. "The armor they are wearing indicates they are ready for war."

"For a power clearly on the wane, Summer sure is pulling out all the stops to...well, stop us," I said, staring out over all of them.

"They surely realize that failing to succeed at this ritual means the end of them," Lockwood said. "Though I doubt they realize the consequences of their failure."

"Lady Cassandra!" A voice called to me out of the dark and snow; a cold anger washed over me as I recognized it. A faerie near the back of the group had removed his helmet, shaking his golden hair out.

"Aureus," Iona said, gritting her teeth. "That traitor."

"I do not think you realize what is at stake here," he called out to us. "You may think that you can stop us, but you will soon see the power of the Seelie army. We will protect our king. We stand by him."

"This isn't going to work, Aureus," I called back. "Your power transfer is going to blow up in all our faces. And I mean that literally. Kaboom, big explosion. You ever see anything like that in your Netflix binges?"

Apparently that was the wrong thing to say, because Aureus slammed his helmet back onto his head. "You may use your honeyed words from your perfect lips, Lady Cassandra, but to me they echo Gladys. Well, I promise you truly what she promised me: a glorious explosion, one to end all explosions, and curl the very toes with the thrill of power."

"Oh, if only," Iona muttered.

"This is your last warning," Aureus said. "Leave. We will not hold back if you choose to fight."

"Yeah, not gonna happen, pretty boy," said Derrick.

I watched as he hunched his shoulders, his hands clenched into fists. He let out a pained cry as his body hunched over and began to change...just like Jed's. His arms grew, his chest expanded, his snout lengthened. Fur sprouted on his skin, the same cornflower blond as his hair. A tail sprouted from his back as he bent over on all fours.

He turned and looked at me, his blue eyes sharp and full.

"Derrick...?" I muttered. I mean, I should have seen it coming, if I hadn't been so busy with my own problems.

He blinked at me once before leaping off the stairs and into the crowd of knights. He bowled six of them over, showing no mercy as he attacked.

"Wow," Iona said. She looked at me. "Didn't we *save* him from becoming a werewolf?"

I blinked a few times, really not sure that I was seeing what my eyes were telling me I was seeing. "Um, yes. But I guess he decided to go his own way. Back to his roots."

"I told you that boy was lying to you," Orianna said, so very self-satisfied.

"Fight now," Iona said, "gloat later." And she leapt into the fray.

And we followed.

Iona and Xandra found a fight immediately, clashing with and bowling over Fae soldiers with their superior strength. Lockwood and Orianna lit the area with flashes of magic, downing paladins here and there, their magic occasionally bouncing back against the armored, shadowy figures in the snowy dark.

But I found no fight, because every time I'd be about to hit one of them, either Derrick would race ahead and bowl the armored figure over, or Iona would leap in front of me and tackle them, or a spell would send them toddling aside as if struck on the helm by a hammer.

Which was convenient, because I was carrying an improvised weapon consisting of three nails sticking out between the fingers of my balled fist. And these guys were in armor. Where was I supposed to hit them? It didn't seem likely they'd hold still and let me jam the nails into the little face slit in their helmets.

A faerie soldier broke out of the line and swung his sword at me, and I leapt backward. The tip of the sword sang toward me and grazed the front of my jacket, exposing the fluffy, white stuffing inside.

My heart was in my throat. I was going to end up with a hole in me if that sword actually made contact.

I retreated through the knee-deep snow, leaving trails like a wriggling snake through the grass. Moving in this was near-impossible. The soldier, fluttering above it all, struck out at me again. I jumped away. He struck again. I stumbled over my own boots as I tried to move, and it caused me to fall over backward into the snow like I was about to make a snow angel.

I stared up at the soldier, who let out a low cackle, and quickly rolled to the side to avoid the blade that he had brought down over his head. It slammed into the snow right where I had been laying, sending a puff flying into the air.

Sensing my one and only opportunity, I threw myself at the soldier's leg. I struck, nails just glancing off the metal plating.

Fail. Epic fail.

My heart was beating rapidly. My breathing was ragged and harsh, the cold air burning my lungs every time I breathed it in. I was rolling sideways over the snow, half crawling, anything I had to do to get away.

I was used to fighting vampires, enemies that I could get close to. As long as these soldiers had their swords, they would be able to keep me at a distance.

I was going to have to change my tactics.

Otherwise, I was going to get nothing more than a sword between my ribs – and Tampa would be destroyed.

41

"Yield, Lady Cassandra," said the paladin, his voice muffled by the helmet as he fluttered closer, sword in hand, beating wings stirring up the snow. "You are a valiant fighter, but against the might of Summer you are outmatched."

My eyes narrowed. "If so-called Summer was that mighty, we wouldn't be fighting in six inches of snow."

The faerie did not respond but to swing his sword again, almost catching me off guard. My stomach dropped as the blade grazed the wrist of my coat. I barely had time to scramble away. The skin on the back of my hand stung, wet blood sliding down my wrist as I clasped my hand to my chest.

He raised his weapon to strike the killing blow, and there was nothing to stop him. A blur of purple came from his side, slamming into him and he went flying like he'd been struck by a car. Xandra resolved out of the blur, snowflakes flying all around her. She dusted her hands off, grinning at me.

"Thanks," I said, letting out a breath I didn't know I was holding. "Feel like I'm fighting in a bisque here."

"But without the deliciousness," Xandra said, helping me up. She made a face. "Is it wrong that I kinda want a blood bisque?"

I made a face of my own, much more disgusted. "Normally I would say 'yes' because that's nasty. But...you're a vamp now. Accommodations must be made. And honestly, I think your dietary restrictions are still more reasonable than dealing with someone who's both vegan and gluten free." I looked at the claws in between my fingers. "I really am not doing a lot of good up here."

"Why don't we team up?" Xandra said. "You know, now that I'm more of an equal partner rather than a liability."

"You've always been an asset to me," I said softly.

Iona seemed to appear out of nowhere. "You guys are doing a team-up without me? Unfair." She gave Xandra a mean look. "Also, I'll have you know I was all set to take over the mantle of best friend, then you had to come back."

"...Sorry?" Xandra didn't seem that sorry; she seemed kind of irritated, the wind blowing her hair as flakes landed in it. Up close, I could see that both Xandra and Iona were flecked with silver faerie blood. Xandra had a good amount of it on her hands, dripping like molten metal from her claw-like nails.

"You should be," Iona said, "but if you help me get revenge on the man who played with my heart like a toy, you're back in and we can all be besties together. Because that's what friends do."

Xandra and I exchanged a look. It was questioning, kind of curious at the very premise of Iona's argument. "Sure," I said. "I suspect we're going to have to face off with Aureus anyway. He seemed pretty much a true believer in this thing."

"Also," Xandra was trying to wipe off some of the faerie blood from her hands, "it's hard to get in a good hit on these guys. They're armored too well."

"Like turtles," Iona said.

"Yes, like turtles with swords and a lot of pent-up anger," Xandra said. "And it takes too long to tear them up enough to stop them. But if one of us can hold them, then Cassie can pop them with her super fun kitty claws."

As if demanding to be a test subject, a knight lurched into our midst, knee deep in the snow rather than flying. He threw himself at me with all the composure of a drunken frat boy at the last unoccupied woman in the room. I jumped aside just as Iona leapt at him, knocking his sword away. Xandra's arm appeared around his neck, cranking him into a headlock.

Seeing my chance, I popped him right in the underside of his jaw with the nails.

I half expected blood to pour out over my hands, but instead, the faerie just sort of exploded like a party favor into sparkles and glitter. It was caught immediately in the wind, and carried away from us like glitter fallout.

"All right," Xandra said, clapping her hands, little sparkles of glitter coming off them. "Teamwork makes the dream work."

As if sensing a new birth of arrogance from us, the ground beneath us suddenly shook. The sky somehow became darker, and, if possible, the temperature dropped further, the wind howling frigidly through with such viciousness I shivered beneath my heavy jacket.

A wavering blue light glowed above the amphitheater

like a dome. I could just see the top of it, but it was a mass of swirling energy and magic.

"They're starting," I heard Orianna cry over the sound of the now howling wind. The ground gave another tremendous shake.

"We have to get to the amphitheater," I said and, ignoring the rumbling, plunged through the snow toward it.

———————

42

We managed to get around the first line of faeries, and made a beeline to the entrance to the amphitheater. I staggered to a halt as we crested the top of the theater and saw what was happening down on the stage.

The stage had become like a window into a different world. Magic crackled and light glowed, and in the midst of it I saw the king standing over a stone slab. I recognized the long, shining hair of the Summer Queen laid out like Aslan on the slab. A few others were crowded in there as well, magic pouring from their hands and adding to the giant spell. It was obviously fueling the dome, which seemed to be expanding, pulsating and wavering as it did. They looked like they were standing in a snowy meadow somewhere. Occasionally the image would flicker, and then they seemed to be on the stage.

Portal, doorway, glaring problem. It wasn't stable, whatever it was.

"I'm no expert on magic–" Xandra said.

"Or anything, except anime," Iona said.

"–but this does not look under control," Xandra said. "Look at the king's face."

She was right; the king's expression was strained and tight, his teeth gritted painfully. His hands shook as magic poured out of them, like a flow that seemed to be both coming into the queen and out of her, as well.

"Lady Cassandra," called Aureus's voice again. He stood with another group of knights below us in the amphitheater, all of whom were bigger, taller, and even meaner looking than the first group of knights. Their armor was as white as the snow, and their helmets were in the shape of an eagle's head, with a long, pointed beak and metal feathers fanning out from the sides as if they were flying.

"Those are seasoned Paladins, Cassandra," Lockwood said, flitting in to land behind us, Orianna a step behind him. "The very best there is."

An icy sickness filled my stomach. "They're standing between us and stopping the end of the world."

"And there they will remain," Lockwood said. "They have sworn their loyalty to the king. They will die for him."

"Their loyalty is a fickle thing," Iona said. "Didn't they swear loyalty to the queen before that? You know, the one that's being murdered behind them as we speak?"

"I'm sure they don't see it that way," I said. The cold wind came through so heavy that it was stinging my cheeks. My toes had gone numb inside my boots, and my fingers were having a hard time moving. I stuffed them into my armpits, but my body was trying to keep as much heat inside as possible. This was beyond New York in January. It was becoming deadly. "We don't have time for this."

"We have all the time in the world," Aureus called back. "The Summer Queen has ruined our lands. Despoiled our pride. You, humans – you should understand this. You threw off your tyrants and chose your own rulers."

"Did he just 1776 us?" Xandra asked. Beside her, Derrick growled. I hadn't even heard him arrive.

"You need to get to the king," Lockwood said, hovering just behind me, talking in a soft voice. "Let the rest of us deal with these soldiers."

"If they see me, I'm screwed," I muttered back. Aureus was monologuing about the "repeated injuries and usurpations" that the Summer Fae had suffered at the hands of the queen; whether a pocket copy of the Declaration of Independence had been one of the items to accidentally wash into Faerie or he'd discovered one on Gladys's shelves while avoiding her probing hands, I neither knew nor cared.

"You're the knife in the back," Lockwood murmured. "We will be the sword they are forced to guard against."

"I'm ready to be a sword," Xandra said.

"Are you ready to take one?" Iona asked. "Hypothetically. For the team. When I push you on one, I mean." Xandra shot her an alarmed, questioning look. "Accidentally. Partially accidentally. But slightly on purpose."

"Go," Lockwood said, and jetted up, Orianna moving beside him. They showered blasts of magic at the offensive line of the Summer Paladins, interrupting Aureus in the midst of a particularly moving rant about the right of the people to abolish their government. Derrick plunged into the midst of them, bowling over several of them as he howled. Iona and Xandra followed, working in concert.

As soon as the line of Fae were occupied, I bolted to the side, plodding through the snow drifts covering the seats in the amphitheater. I descended, trying to get down to the stage, where the magic was surging.

The dome portal was getting bigger by the minute, the power and magic pooling together in a coruscating effect. The explosion seemed to be building, and the king and his courtiers neither knew – nor cared – that the only thing they were really courting at the moment was the death of us all.

43

I made it to the bottom step, only feet from the king and the dome, when Aureus slid in front of me, his armor gleaming in the magical glow. His wings fluttered in the light, and he hovered there, blocking my path.

"Let me through," I said. My hands were numb, my back muscles ached from shivering, or from trying to suppress the shivers. It hurt to breathe. My eyes had dried out, and I was having a hard time keeping them moist, no matter how much I blinked. Were my tears freezing? Frost had started to form on my eyelashes and eyebrows, making them heavy.

"No." Aureus seemed like he was not doing much better, swinging his sword in front of himself as if to draw a line in the sand. "I cannot let you interfere, Lady Cassandra. My people need to be free."

Iona was suddenly at my side. She gave me a once-over. "Your eyelashes are freezing. Who's Elsa now?"

"Stand aside," Aureus said. "The purest magic of Faerie runs through our veins, giving us the ancient power of our lands." He shook his head almost sadly. "You cannot hope to defeat the Knights of Summer."

Iona's eyes narrowed, and a devilish look passed over her face. "Is that so?" Without warning, she dashed at him, yanking him down as he tried to flutter away. Manhandling him mercilessly, she buried her mouth in his neck.

I wanted to make a joke about how she needed to stop giving him a hickey, but he screamed in pain, so I shut up.

A few seconds later, Iona shoved him away. He staggered and fell to his knees on the snowy ground. She wiped her mouth with the back of her hand. When she turned and looked at me, and her eyes were sparkling gold and glowing. "I feel...so very magical."

She sprinted behind me, slamming into the Paladin that Xandra was fighting. He went flying, limbs and wings flailing, disappearing over the wall of the amphitheater into the swirling snowstorm like he'd been blasted out of a cannon.

"Holy crap," I said. "You're like, super charged now."

"You just blasted that guy off like Team Rocket," Xandra said. "Whatever you ate, did you save any for me?"

"Get your own dinner," Iona said, silvery blood dripping from her fangs. Her eyes were like little beacons.

"Fine, I will," Xandra said. She threw herself at a faerie knight that was tangoing with Lockwood, grabbed him by the back of the neck and sunk her own teeth into his neck.

When she came up, Xandra's eyes were glowing, too. She and Iona grinned at each other like some sort of crazed, bloodthirsty beasts. Then they both turned their attention to Aureus, who had gotten, a bit wobbly, to his feet. "No, please," said Aureus. "I am just trying to serve my king, to rescue my people from the dishonor that the queen brought upon us–"

They didn't give him a chance to finish.

It was a flurry of blows, the sound of vampire claws against shrieking metal, and the metal sounded like it was losing. A noise like a can being opened filled the air above Kiley Garden with a wrenching squeal, and below that someone was muttering, low and angry: "You broke my heart, you gorgeous, devilish piece of–"

"Broke your heart?" Xandra asked, looking at Iona. "How long have you known this guy?"

"A day," Iona said, her voice stern as she continued to cave in Aureus's metal chestplate. It was showing serious signs of strain. She must have caught a look from Xandra, because she added: "What? I'm a fairytale princess, clearly. It only takes one day for me to fall in love."

I staggered as the wind suddenly picked up again. I wrapped my arms more tightly around myself. It was at the point that it was so cold that I just couldn't feel a difference any longer, even though I knew it had to be dropping still. Would this be cold enough to freeze the Gulf of Mexico? How far was this destruction spreading?

Aureus was occupied. My way to the king was open. I hurried past them to the edge of the dome.

I could see the stage, then a moment later the dome flickered and a snowy meadow replaced it as backdrop. The king was standing above the Summer Queen, a black sword pressed to her chest. Golden blood was welling out from her sternum, staining the front of her dress and the table beneath her.

"Oh, good," I muttered. "A human – err, Fae – sacrifice."

Her eyes were screwed shut with pain, her fingers were limp at her sides as if the rest of her body was paralyzed.

There were three other people there on the stage with the king, underneath the dome, all robed. I couldn't hear anything, but I saw the king yell something at one of the others. He was still trying to force the blade farther into her.

One of the robed Fae stepped away from the group, and

made their way toward me. I realized quickly that it was a woman, as she tossed the hood back. Golden hair flowed down like molten gold, and she stepped out of the dome as if passing through the mist.

She wasn't armed, so I took the chance and lunged at her, catching her off guard. Her eyes widened; she must have expected me to cower in fear of her. Her hands were raised as if summoning a spell, but I managed to nick her shoulder with a nail-claw before she could do much more than produce a faint glow.

Noiselessly, she burst into golden glitter and was swept away like dust on the winds. Everyone on the stage turned and looked at me as a magic ripple blew through the area, turning the stage to the snowy meadow and back again in a flash. The other two robed figures looked up, the magic flowing from their hands seeming to give them some sort of blowback that staggered them back a step.

With them distracted, I saw my chance, and I stepped forward toward the king and his raised sword, determined to stop him before he murdered his queen – and with her, the world.

44

I was just about to step inside the dome of magic when one of the other spell casters recovered enough to lunge toward me. He had already conjured a ball of brilliant red light, and before I had a chance to close the distance between us, he lobbed it at me. I ducked just in time. The light struck the concrete seats behind me, shattering it as if it had been struck with a cannonball. A spray of concrete chips pelted me, making me feel fortunate it hadn't hit my head. Or my chest.

Circling around, dodging as he threw one after another, I was awash in a blast of concrete chips and blowing snow. Moving sideways against the howling wind was my only defense. I had to stop to give another blast a chance to land, then I was moving again, fighting to get close enough to stop the guy as he threw spell after spell at me.

Another came plowing past, singeing my jacket sleeve. It melted a long stretch of snow on the ground, exposing the sun-faded concrete beneath it. I toppled over, already off balance when I hit a patch of snow. Landing hard, I felt my breath leave me and realized I was defenseless against the Fae wizard's spells.

A flash of fur breezed past, and Derrick leapt from the upper seats down onto the wizard, knocking him down with his two front paws. There was a roar of Derrick-wolf (Derewolf?) and the Fae screamed.

The other wizard was staring at me with wide eyes, sweat beading on his forehead. He was managing the entire dome of magic now, and the strain was showing. The king was still trying as hard as he could to push the sword into the queen's chest. Silvery light was swirling around the blade now, though whether that was his magic or the queen's resisting him, I didn't know.

I stepped underneath the dome, and the whole world around me went quiet. I could no longer hear the sounds of the blizzard, of my friends fighting the Paladins. There was no howling wind. It was all almost peaceful. Almost.

We were in the meadow that I had seen fleeting views of from outside the dome. The ground beneath me was filled with little flowers, all of which were dusted with a powdery, sugary snow. It might have been beautiful...save for the queen sprawled out across the table with a blade through her chest.

The king's head snapped up at my approach, a wild look on his face. He gripped the blade, putting all of his weight on it. He didn't look anything like I remembered; his once handsome face was screwed up in rage, teeth bared like some kind of rabid animal. "Get back, you wretched creature," he spat at me.

"I can't do that," I said. "You're going to destroy us all. You can't handle her mantle."

Apparently that was the wrong choice of words, because his face purpled and he pushed even harder.

The queen let out a pitiful sort of whimper. Her eyes were turned toward me, and growing dim. All her kingdom and all her servants, and she was relying on me to save her from her own husband.

"Why are you doing this?" I asked, trying to calm him down. "I mean, I get that things are maybe not working out for you, but have you considered a divorce? It's what normal people do when their relationship goes south. Keeps you out of trouble for the whole murder thing."

"Death is the only way," the king said, clearly in his right mind. "The Seelie people deserve more than what their queen has provided." The king's breath was forming clouds in front of him, and I realized that his shoulders were trembling with the cold, or the exertion of trying to impale his wife.

"You have to stop this," I said. "You cannot contain this magic. It's going to destroy both our worlds."

"You have no business speaking to the king so informally," the wizard said, though it came out as more of a grunt. He was straining to keep up the spells he was casting. His magic wavered, and he looked like he was trying to hold something up into the air that was too heavy for him. I figured that if he dropped the spells to try and attack me, this whole tear in reality would likely disappear.

"You don't know what I'm capable of," the king said, struggling against the burst of silver light that was trying to encircle the blade. The table shuddered, and he staggered. "She has had the chance to do so much, and in turn has done so little. You saw her lies for yourself, how she was willing to go to any length to maintain the deceit."

Well, he had a point there.

"So that means you need to kill her?" I asked.

"It means that she is undeserving of the world-changing

power that she has squandered." He gave another shove on the sword, and a bright golden light shot out of the queen's abdomen. "And I mean to set it right." The queen gave another cry as more blood spurted from the wound.

It was hard to watch. My stomach was churning, the bile rising in my throat. But I couldn't just charge him – yet. "What you are trying to do is impossible," I said. I wasn't sure if he didn't hear me or if he just didn't want to acknowledge.

The wizard was struggling even more. After that most recent burst of light from the sword, the swirling magic overhead was even more erratic. Blasts of lightning were shooting outward now, fanning into the sky above like they were striking for the clouds. Flakes of snow were illuminated like stop-animation.

"You lack the imagination to see the possible," said the king. "I will bring this magic under my control, and I shall allow the Seelie to experience the change they have so desperately needed. Now – I am done wasting my energy on you. I hope that you have made peace with your life, human. For today is the last day that you will walk this Earth." He snapped his fingers.

As if he were a magnet, golden armor appeared and attached itself to the king as if he were Iron Man. Within seconds he was suited up like his knights.

"Well...crap," I said, looking down at the little puny nails that were poking between my fingers.

"Take up my part," the king said to the wizard, nodding to the sword. "We can ill afford any more interruptions." The wizard slipped into place and took it up before the king removed his own. The queen writhed beneath it, the wizard holding it steady while the King stalked out around the stone table toward me, his footsteps crushing the delicate, snow-covered flowers beneath his feet. He held his hand out at his side, and a glow of green emanated from his palm. It solidified into a sword, and a green blade that was as clear as glass.

If I wasn't a little worried, I might have thought it was really cool.

"I so hate snuffing out the light of life, especially given that your actions have brought us this opportunity," said the king, "but I must put my people first, even before you. I hope you understand."

I swallowed nervously, all of my limbs still slow and stiff from the cold.

This was the king himself. The way he held the sword and the way that he stood in his armor told me all that I needed to know; he was well-trained, a seasoned warrior.

I was just some teenage girl who had gotten lucky a few times against some vampires. I stared at the blade, wondering if finally, this was going to be the thing that ended me.

Well, at least it would be over fast. Of course, being stabbed probably wouldn't be as quick as being vaporized in a magical explosion.

Alas.

45

I slid backward into the snowy meadow, keeping my eyes on the king. I had no idea if I would be able to leave the dome, let alone leave this little pocket of Faerie he'd brought into the middle of Tampa. I had nothing aside from the dumb Wolverine claw things in my hands. And with his armor, there was no way that I was going to get any kind of hit on him.

His golden eagle helm turned toward me, the plumage of brilliant feathers a striking contrast to the alabaster snow around us.

I heard a clink of armor behind me, and wheeled around to see another set of golden armor coming toward me, snow crunching beneath his feet.

My heart sank. Great. One of them got through Xandra and Iona. Because facing the king and his sword wasn't already enough. Hopefully the two of them were at least all right.

The soldier stopped right behind me, and looked down at me. The soldier's sword was slate blue, with a pearly sort of appearance. It reminded me of–

The face plate slid open, and I exhaled, relief washing over me.

"Lockwood," I said. He nodded at me with a small, affectionate smile, but his attention was primarily on the king.

"Paladin," said the king. "You were stripped of your rank and forbidden to return to the Seelie court."

"I am not in the Seelie court," Lockwood said. "This is neutral territory." His eyebrows were a storm cloud beneath his helm. "In spite of this visual trick, you are on my ground, now – and I suggest you leave."

"I do not bow to the whims of traitors." The king made a noise of disgust and swung his sword.

"You have usurped a throne that is not yours," Lockwood said, his voice low and dark. He raised his blade in response, and stepped between the king and me, giving me a gentle push backward. "You are destroying Faerie." Their swords clashed with a sound like thunder beyond the dome. "You are attempting to take something that is not rightly yours. This is basest thievery."

The dome around us wavered, and suddenly I could see the park in Tampa again. I turned around and saw Iona and Xandra wrestling another guard to the ground, moving in fast forward like someone had sped up film, both drenched in silver blood.

I froze as I heard a rush behind me, and realized just in time that the magic dome disappearing must mean that the wizard gave up attempting to hold onto the spell and was making a dash at me. I leapt to the side in time to avoid his charge, dodging around the queen and the table, putting her between me and the wizard.

The dome had disappeared, but the magic was still spiraling out of control. It was shooting upward from the blade embedded in the queen's chest. Beams of brilliant colors, all swirling overhead and coruscating over the thick clouds above. The wind was howling still, and the snow was still falling thick and fast, lit by the colorful magic like a strobe. The last wizard was circling, trying to maintain the magic of the dome with one hand while using the other to conjure a spell to kill me.

I had to get rid of him. I had to break the connection between Faerie and Earth. And he was the key to doing so. I ducked behind the stone slab just as he lobbed a white-hot ball of fire at me. The hair on the top of my head fluttered as it just missed me.

There was a murmur from behind me. I looked up at the slab to see the queen's finger index finger twitch. Ever so slightly, it lifted from the rest of her hand, and...pointed?

I looked in the direction of her point and saw what looked like a dagger sticking out of the snow. It was a dark metal, and looked more like a tooth from a huge shark than a blade. Scurrying through the snow, trying to keep low, I grabbed the hilt. Better than my measly nails, at least. As I lifted it up...it was heavy. Almost as if it were made of cast iron.

Then I realized: it probably was. To a faerie, this weapon would be way more deadly than anything else he would have been up against. It wasn't even all that sharp, and it had a rough surface just like my mom's cast iron pans.

The wizard saw me holding it, and he hesitated before throwing the next spell at me.

"Do your worst," I said, hurrying around the slab toward him. The dagger was almost like a shield, too, as big as a hand mirror with its tooth-shaped blade. The wizard tossed the magic at me, and I held the dagger out in front.

It was absorbed into the blade like water into a sponge, the red light diffusing like it had never even exited.

The wizard's face paled, his mouth opening in shock as he readied another spell.

I was closing the gap between us as he tossed another spell at me. He tried to aim around the blade, but I moved it like I was playing a giant game of ping pong, and *zap!* His spell disappeared leaving nothing more than a slight char smell.

"No, wait," shouted the wizard, recoiling as I advanced on him. "I have a family." He held up his hands weakly.

"Lots of people have families," I said, regret pulling at my heart for what was about to happen. "And you were about to destroy a whole lot of them."

"Fine." His face hardened into a mask of anger, and he generated another blast of magic that he hurled at me, though it was absorbed into the cast iron. "Have it your way, Iron Bearer. I know now that it is not merely your weapon that is iron, but your very heart–"

I rammed the blade into his chest, the glow of his last spell still fading off of it. He hadn't tried to run. "If one of us has a heart of iron," I said, feeling a little sick from what I'd just done, "it's not me."

He stared at me, stunned, for just a moment and then the world flickered, the stage at Kiley Garden reappearing for just a moment. He burst into glitter and was gone, thankfully, because I'd already seen what iron did to a Faerie in their own world once before, and I had no desire to watch it blacken and burn his skin off before my very eyes. I had enough on my conscience this week already, given that I'd killed a human thrall.

There was a thump behind me and I whirled to find a gold-clad knight lying helmet-less upon the stage, his hair spilling out onto the stone stage. "I surrender," he moaned, lifting his head.

It was Aureus, beaten and bloodied, a steady flow of his silvery blood threatening to pour out of his neck. He had no weapon and seemed to be focused on staunching the wound, coughing tearily.

"I accept your surrender," Iona said, striding up to follow. She'd thrown him down from the cheap seats and he'd punched right through the dome, which was already starting to fade, in spite of the magic still flowing out of the queen and the sword in her chest. "Though I have to admit," and she wiped her mouth of some of the Fae blood, "part of me was hoping you wouldn't."

Aureus moaned. "This world is too savage for me, with your seagulls, and your vampires, and Gladys."

Orianna fluttered down beside me, placing a delicate hand on my shoulder. "Look – Lockwood."

I looked. Lockwood was battering aside the king's every attack like the seasoned Paladin he was. However long it had been since he'd put on his armor, it was clearly not as long as it had been for the king. The blue blade met the green, and the king's was knocked aside.

"You think your actions serve Faerie?" The king was gasping, and lifted his blade slowly. His armor, so impressive, was dotted with Fae blood, the result of Lockwood tearing him to pieces one blow at a time. The King's movements showed he was sapped, barely able to lift his sword. "That putting this unworthy cow back on the throne will make things right?"

"What makes you any more worthy?" Lockwood asked, barely breathing hard. "You try to take by low force what you could not earn on your own, what you could not handle were you even given it. Your ambition may spring from a noble place, but it would lead us all into death." He struck a glancing hit against the king's side, but somehow found the gap in his armor as the king tried to guard, and failed. Another welling of silvery blood sprung from the gap, running down the golden armor. "You may be trying to do good, but you do evil."

"Also," Xandra said, stepping up beside Iona, her purple hair blowing in the furious wind, "killing your wife? Pretty low, bro."

"She deserves what came to her," the king said, barely able to lift his sword. Lockwood had bled him out, truly. His voice was tinged with spite. "The power should have been mine." He looked at me. "All of it."

I was already stepping forward, unwilling to let Lockwood finish this one, given all that this man had done to ruin my night – and almost my world. "Unfortunately for you, by the laws of the State of Florida, you're really only entitled to half."

He cocked his head at me, and his helm visor dropped, clanking, one of the hinges damaged by Lockwood's attacks choosing that moment to fail. The king seemed not to notice, staring at me blankly. "...What?"

"It's called a divorce," I said, slamming the cast iron blade into the gap of his armor just below his waist. Lockwood joined me, ramming his own home at the king's neck. "I'd tell you to look it up, but...I kinda think you're past that now."

Magic swirled around us again, the scene flickering back and forth between the snowy meadow and the stage in Kiley Garden. Darkness reigned, split asunder by the glow of the spell as the queen reached up, no longer immobilized, and seized hold of the blade in her chest.

"Now...you are stuck with her," the king said, a line of slow burn rising up his face – then, as the background changed back to the gardens, he exploded into golden glitter–

The queen ripped the blade out of herself like some sort of Fae King Arthur, and a blast of magic exploded out in its wake. Gone was Kiley Garden, gone was the stage, and – as my friends were knocked off their feet by the blast of the spell coming to its terrible end–

Gone was the night. Sun shone down on the snowy meadow, warming my face, and my cold fingers, and–

Oh, no.

Turning my head, I saw Xandra and Iona laid out on the snow-covered ground–

And the sun was shining down on them.

46

"NOOOO!" I shouted, throwing myself at them. The sun of Faerie beat down on the twin vampires, the clouds blown away and the darkness ripped asunder by the end of the king's spell. Iona blinked up at the blinding light, her pale, angelic face lit by its glow. Xandra, too, was turning to look at it, and I could feel death coming for both of them.

I'd just gotten Xandra back and I was about to lose her again. My chest felt like I'd just buried the cast iron blade in my heart.

Landing on them, I tried to stretch myself across their faces, their exposed skin. "We need to get you out of the light," I shouted, trying to block them from the sun, to give them shade.

"Cassie," Iona said, giving me a gentle shove. "I am not on fire."

Xandra squinted up into the sunlight around me. "Clearly we are not in Kansas anymore."

"I thought you were from Tampa," Aureus said, muffled from where he was lying face down.

I got off my vampire besties, and caught a very amused

look from Iona. "Thank you for trying to save me," she said, dripping irony, "by smothering me."

"You don't breathe, I can't smother you," I said, unzipping my jacket. Ten seconds in the sun of Faerie and I was already sweating. The snow was melting around us. I glanced about and saw my whole squad had made it – Derrick was back to human, and I hadn't even realized he'd been wearing a speedo under his jeans. Now it was all he was wearing, and I swiftly looked away.

I was the only one, though. "Hm," Iona said, bringing a prodigious amount of eye contact into the moment. Uncomfortably much, in fact.

"You already lost your potential boyfriend for the day," Xandra said. Apparently she'd lost some inhibitions by becoming a vampire.

The Summer Queen had managed to sit up on the stone slab, blood dripping down her front. She cast the sword aside, and was staring hard at someone standing only feet away–

Oh. It was the Winter Queen, I realized, with her raven hair and ice blue eyes. She seemed to be weaving a spell of ice that was floating from her fingers like the strings of a marionette puppet. It took me a second to realize she was mending the Summer Queen's wounds. She seemed very intent on her work, keeping her lips tightly shut as she worked.

"There," the Winter Queen said eventually. The magic at her fingertips faded away, and she lowered her hands. "That should at least keep you from losing any more blood. Your own healers will be able to treat you more thoroughly when you are returned to your territory."

"If I have any loyal ones left," the Summer Queen said bitterly, her fingers grazing the hole in her dress. The dried, cracked blood on her sternum was appalling, like old paint. With a furtive look she muttered, "Thank you."

"You need not thank me." The Winter Queen folded her arms over her chest in a way more graceful way than I ever could. "Saving you was as act of self-preservation, not beneficence."

"And yet what was your healing if not charity?" the Summer Queen asked. "Mercy and pity for the betrayed."

The Winter Queen made a disappointed sort of grunt. "Perhaps I saw a bit of my own fate reflected in yours. A simple mirror to a future that might have been for me."

"Y'all need better husbands, if this is a valid fear for both of you," Xandra said, then shoved her hands over her mouth. "Sorry. I'm a vampire now, and apparently my filter went bye-bye along with my heartbeat."

"Such curious made from this event," the Summer Queen said. "And my power has returned, so your...filter...is immaterial." She raised her chin. "I owe all of you much thanks, from the lowest," and here she looked rather pointedly at Derrick, "to the high." And here she nodded at the Winter Queen...and finally, Lockwood. "Whatever your purposes, you have done me a good turn. If it be in my power to return this favor owed, then it shall be done."

"I need no favor," the Winter Queen said, "save that you perhaps allow me the courtesy of taking up your place in the firmament once more." She gestured vaguely around the snowy field. "The signs of my season are all about – replacing it with the signs of yours would be for the best, I think."

The Summer Queen's eyes narrowed, but with a wave of her hand, the snow melted and meadow was restored. Bright, warm sunlight filtered down through the trees overhead. Flowers of purple and yellow and pink and pale blue sprung to life, all pointed happily upward. The air smelled fresh and clean, as if it had just rained.

"With this transfer of power, I must recede," said the Winter Queen, and curtsied to the Summer Queen. "By your leave, I take mine."

The Summer Queen stood proudly, and nodded, her shoulders tense as she watched the Winter Queen walk away. I could easily believe the Summer Queen was pleased to be rid of her opposite number. She was probably humiliated and ashamed enough as it was, having to be rescued by the other, opposite power in Faerie.

"I should follow my sovereign," Orianna said, taking a step toward the exit of the meadow. "Our season is at its end." Glamour gone, she was back to golden hair, wings, eyes. She gave me a wide grin. "Thank you, Cassie, for everything. If you are ever back in Faerie, make sure to come visit the Winter Court. The queen would love to express her gratitude for your aid and hospitality."

The Summer Queen folded her arms over her chest, making an impatient sigh.

"Thank you, too, Orianna," I said with a smile. For some reason, as much as she annoyed me, it made me sad to see her go. "If I'm ever in the neighborhood, I'll make sure to stop by." I looked her over; she was still wearing my favorite outfit. "Any chance I can have that back before you go?"

She looked wounded, but shed it immediately. It looked weird over her golden Fae attire anyway.

With a last look at Lockwood she stuck out her tongue. "I don't hate you anymore, Summer Paladin."

Lockwood seemed unsure how to take this, but she was gone and out of the meadow before he could get any words out. "Same goes," he said at last, though quietly.

"Yeah, that should probably be our cue to go, too," I said,

looking at the others. The Summer Queen was just standing there, silently, but I could feel her judgmental eyes upon me and I was starting to worry she might smite me just for the heck of it.

"You," she said, looking right at me. "You are free to traverse my lands as you please. You and your vassals. As long as you bring no threat here, then none will be visited upon you."

Wow, that was more than I expected from her, especially after everything that had happened the last time we had met in person. I half expected her to cast us out of Faerie right then and there.

"As for me, I must reclaim my throne," she said with a heavy sigh. "And reconstitute my court." She turned and looked at Lockwood. Her expression softened. "My Paladin of Summer...I thought your loyalty broken, yet only you of all my servants returned to save me. And through your curious choice in friends, you have saved our kingdom. I would welcome you home," she said, her voice gentle, and a small smile appearing on her tired face.

Lockwood inclined his head at her. "And also Earth."

"Of course," she said, and her smile faded. "Still...you are welcome back at your position within the Seelie Court if ever your heart calls you home. It will be waiting here for you should life on Earth grow dull."

There was a twinge of anger in me, and also of fear. Lockwood leave? I didn't like the idea of that.

"Thank you, my Queen," said Lockwood, bowing his head. "May your reign never end."

"May that be so," she said. Then she turned and looked down at Aureus laid out upon the ground. Beaten, bleeding, humiliated, it had been a hell of a comedown for the golden-haired Summer Knight. "And you," she said, sounding more disgusted than angry, "I am tempted to give you over to these blood drinkers for their own amusement."

"Wait, she's going to give him to us?" Xandra asked, elbowing Iona in the ribs. Iona, for her part, did not seem eager to receive this gift. "Can we keep him? Like to feed off of or something?"

Iona shot her the most revolted look. "What are you trying to suggest with the 'or something?'"

I gave Xandra the most caustic look. "You need to work on this vampire morality thing, because that is either Fae ranching, pimping, or slavery depending on your answer."

"I'm just trying to plan ahead for the future," Xandra said. "I know I'm gonna need to eat, and I gotta tell you, going to human blood after that–" and she pointed at Aureus, "–is like driving a rusted out station wagon after you've taken a Ferrari for a spin. Also – I don't want to kill people. And he's not a people."

"I am afraid this I cannot give you." The queen reached down and grabbed Aureus by the back of his neck, just like Iona had. "Come, my purported servant. It is time that we had a conversation about where your loyalties truly lie."

"I am all right with whatever punishment you devise, my Queen," Aureus gasped out, his lips bloody and fear etched on every line of his face, "so long as you do not send me back...to Gladys."

"Then to Gladys I may very well send you," the queen said, and his face, seemingly so earnest, became lined with shock. "Whoever she is." And then she departed without another glance in our direction, without a goodbye, leaving us standing there alone in the flowery, sunny meadow as she dragged Aureus to his fate.

47

"Well, I guess we should be getting back home," I said, looking across the multi-colored meadow of flowers. I'd unzipped my jacket, because it was getting really warm, and sweat was coursing under my winter gear. "I don't know about any of you, but I am so tired I could sleep standing up right now." As if to illustrate the point, I started to drift sideways. Derrick caught me with a bare arm and I blushed as I moved to stand upright. "Also...I think I'm melting, and I don't have ruby slippers to click together."

Iona frowned. "Isn't it midmorning back on Earth? Xandra and I can't go back if there's sunlight."

"Oh, right," I said, and looked over at Lockwood.

"The problem is the timing," Lockwood said, looking pensive.

"Obviously," Xandra said. "Can't we just wait until it gets dark and then cross over?"

I understood what Lockwood meant. "Time passes differently here in Faerie. Last time I was here for almost a week, and only like five minutes passed on Earth."

"Wait," Iona said. "We're going to be stuck here in Faerie for *weeks* until night falls in our world?"

Lockwood nodded. "If we leave from this place, yes. There are other places we could cross over where the time relationship is less...slow...but they are some distance away."

"How far?" Xandra asked.

Lockwood shrugged. "A week and a half, perhaps. But through some quite impressive scenery, if I do say so."

Xandra and Iona exchanged a look. "Great," Iona said. "Stuck in a sunny wonderland with anime kitty."

Xandra, however, had her face turned up toward the sun. "How bad would a few weeks in the sun really be for us, you know? I, for one, really like it, even if it hates me now. On our planet, at least."

"So we might as well get going, right?" Derrick said. "If we have weeks to travel."

"I was talking about the vampires, only," Lockwood said. "I can take you and Cassandra home now, as the sun affects you not."

I looked at Derrick, and then back at the vampires, a bit dazedly. "Would you guys be okay with that?"

"Lady Cassandra, may I interject?" Lockwood said. "They will be fine with me. You, on the other hand, look as though you are about to collapse."

"How long has it been since you slept, Cassie?" Xandra asked, studying my face. "Before my funeral, right?"

"Longer," I said, because I hadn't slept in over a day, and hadn't slept well since...

"Cass..." I heard Xandra say in a low, sad voice. She knew.

"Okay," I said, realizing I was still leaning on Derrick. I felt a little like I was underwater. "I'll go home. And I'll see you two...in a few weeks, I guess?"

"We'll see you tonight, by your reckoning," Xandra said, and Lockwood nodded approvingly. "Get some sleep." She leaned in and gave me a hug. "I'm glad that we are back together. And...I'm really sorry that I put you through so much stress and pain. I promise that I will try to make it up."

My heart clenched in my chest. "I have a lot more to make up for," I said. "I'm the one that caused it all."

"Stop it," Xandra said. "No more guilt tripping, okay? I love you. You're my very best friend." She kissed me on the cheek. "Also, now that I've tasted Faerie blood, you no longer smell like food to me. Which is great news."

I laughed and hugged her back. "Love you, too. And I'm so relieved you lost your appetite for my blood."

"I just want it said for the record," Iona said, her amber eyes flashing brightly in the sunlight of Faerie, "I never thought of you as a food source, which is why I should be your best friend. Also, I'm not even mad that you've brought me to a place it's going to take weeks to escape. With no cars. Where I'm just going to have to walk the land like Caine in *Kung Fu*. Because forgiveness is what best friends do." And she hugged me, but it was way more awkward than Xandra's.

"Is everyone ready?" Lockwood asked. Without any further ado, he snapped his fingers, and the three of us were back on Earth, back in Kiley Garden, looking up at the skyscrapers of Tampa.

The first thing I noticed were the birds singing. The sun was shining down, just as hot and as potent as any other summer day. The amphitheater was slick with melted snow, and I realized that all of the evidence of our fight had gone, too. Either the Fae had all turned to glitter or they'd been sucked back into Faerie when the spell broke.

Lockwood turned to me. He was glamoured again, and

wearing a pair of blue jeans and an Oakleys T-shirt with a pair of sunglasses on. "Lady Cassandra," he said, taking a deep breath and looking out over the river beside us. "You have done it again."

"Yay, gratitude." Derrick stood there in nothing but his speedo. His bare feet slopped against the wet concrete. "Can we get moving? This isn't Miami, I feel like I'm going to stand out."

Lockwood nodded. "You never cease to impress me. Uh...her, not you." He reached into the pocket of his jeans and handed Derrick the keys to the SUV. "Please see her home safely. And try not to get arrested for your attire."

Derrick snatched them out of his hands. "My pants are around here somewhere, okay? I'll find them." And he stalked off.

"Take care of yourself, Lady Cassandra," Lockwood said. Before I could muster a reply, he snapped his fingers, and I was alone in the park with the melting snow.

———————

48

"So I'm guessing you're waiting for me to tell you what's been going on with the wolf thing, huh?" Derrick asked. He was at the wheel of Lockwood's SUV, wearing his snow-wet clothes, window down on the warm day, sun drying him.

"No," I said, barely awake.

Derrick was quiet for a minute, and then looked over at me.

"I'm going to tell you anyway," he said. "After what happened with Xandra and those vamps...I felt pathetic. Like a coward–"

"Derrick–"

"You won't convince me otherwise," he said, sandy blond hair shining in the light of the Tampa sun. Now that the snow was melting, people were out on the streets, emerging as if from hibernation. "That night, after we made it out – after you saved us – I kept thinking if my dad had succeeded in changing me, then maybe the fight would have turned out different..."

I remained silent as he took a minute to gather his thoughts.

"I mean, look at you," he said. "You're a human, and you keep going into these crazy situations, and you're no stronger than I was. But really...you're brave. And I just wasn't."

"I would never think," I said slowly, trying to make the words come out right, not slurring from my tiredness, "that anyone was a coward or not brave because they chose to sit out on the things I've gotten myself into. That's sanity, not a lack of courage."

"Maybe," Derrick said. "Maybe not, though. What if you'd decided to be 'sane' today? What would have happened?"

"You may have a point," I said. "But are you sure it was the right choice to make? I mean, it's not like you can go back on this one down the road. They don't have shelters where you can give up the wolf for adoption. I mean, it's in you."

"I have no regrets." He shook his head. "I have purpose now. It's what I never knew I'd always needed."

Purpose. He had found his purpose.

It made me start to wonder...

What was my purpose?

"I understand," I said. "And I admire the desire to become a better person. I just hope that you did this for you, and not for anyone else."

Derrick shook his head. "It was for me. No force, no coercion, no disappointment from my dad. All me. Besides," he ran his fingers through his hair, "I can help you anytime that you need it now. I'm useful."

"You were always useful," I said. "More than useful. You were wanted. Remember that, okay?"

We pulled up outside his house, and he put the car in park. "You sure you want to drive the last mile? I can drop you off."

I shook my head slowly. "I can handle that much. Besides, I want Lockwood to know where to find it."

He grinned at me and hopped out, turning to wave.

I waved back as I slowly made my way to the driver's seat, put the car in drive, and took it nice and easy down the road. "I don't remember him having abs like that at the beach earlier this summer," I muttered as I concentrated on not falling asleep. Being a werewolf made him, uhm...leaner.

I smiled. It was good to have another ally.

But there would be time to think about tactical gains later. For now, I just wanted to go home, sink into my bed, and stay there for the next three days.

Or at least until Xandra and Iona came barreling into my room, filled to the brim with stories about their adventure in Faerie.

I smiled.

I wondered what they were doing at that exact moment, and how much time had already passed.

49

W hen was the last time I had been alone like this? The car was quiet. I had the windows down, letting the warm, salty air in. I watched people brush snow from the hoods of their cars, the last bits of it that hadn't melted yet. There was still snow on the road, and I was terribly drowsy, so I was taking it carefully.

Xandra's grave. That was the last time I'd been alone, I realized. Over twelve hours – and seemingly a lifetime – ago. The best thing about having people around was they did a lot to help keep me awake.

We had saved Tampa, and put a stop to everything that was going wrong in Faerie. But the best thing of all of it was that Xandra was back. And it was really Xandra. A newfound taste for blood, but otherwise...it was her.

I turned the corner into my neighborhood, my heart feeling at peace for the most part. I knew there were going to be issues ahead, a brewing beef with Jacquelyn and Varycas I needed to resolve. And I'd probably have to see Mill again at some point, but for now...

...Things were good. They felt *good*.

"I wonder if Dad would whip me up some pancakes when he gets home," I said to the air, feeling almost giddy at the thought of something so ordinary. "After I finish sleeping..."

The words faded on my lips as I turned onto our street and saw several police cars with their lights flashing right in front of my house.

My stomach dropped. Icy fear swept through my veins as if it were still below freezing outside.

No. No, no, no.

I pulled in behind one of the police cars, almost mounting the curb, and jumped out of the car, not even bothering to turn off the ignition, my mind already jumping to the obvious conclusions.

Jacquelyn. I was going to walk in the house and find their bodies, just like I'd found Xandra's. Cold, lifeless, their eyes staring blankly into eternity. Maybe just Mom. Maybe both of them somehow. Maybe they got Dad at work, dragged him home, forced him to invite them inside...

My stomach heaved, and my legs turned to jelly as I hurried across the lawn.

"I'm sorry, miss, but this is a crime scene," said a police officer who was standing near the front door. He stepped out and blocked my way.

"What happened?" I heard myself say through the facade of adrenaline, the drag of a day and night without sleep. "Where are my parents?"

"Your parents?"

"This is my house," I said. "I need to find my parents. I need to see–" My heart was hammering in my chest, about to explode when I saw Mom's hair over the shoulder of another officer that had just left the house. "Mom!" I cried, lunging toward her.

The officers grabbed me before I could reach her. Handcuffs glittered around her wrists, glaring in the sunlight like Faerie blood. She looked over her shoulder at me as they led her down the front walk toward one of the cars. "It's okay, Cassie," she said, her eyes wide, cheeks sallow. "It's okay, nobody is hurt."

"Is Dad–" I started, tears stinging my eyes.

"Nobody's hurt," Mom said. "Your dad is at work. You have to call him, sweetie. Let him know. It's going to be okay." She tried to smile, but failed. She didn't break eye contact with me until they slipped her into the back of the police car.

I watched them lead my mother away, numbness spreading through me. Having seen what I'd seen, gone through what I had tonight...I was half convinced this was all just some kind of sick joke. Like payback from Aureus, from the King of Summer, or some twisted play by Jacquelyn and Varycas.

But it probably wasn't. This had been coming for a while, and in spite of everything I'd dealt with tonight, somehow this – this dose of reality, away from vampires and Fae and all else – hit harder than anything else.

And I sobbed on my front walk as the police took my mother away.

Cassie Howell Returns in

BURNED ME

Liars and Vampires, Book 9
Coming in 2023!

AUTHOR'S NOTE

Thanks for reading! If you want to know immediately when future books become available, take sixty seconds and sign up for my NEW RELEASE EMAIL ALERTS at my website, www.robertjcrane.com. I don't sell your information and I only send out emails when I have a new book out. The reason you should sign up for this is because I don't always set release dates, and even if you're following me on Facebook (robertJcrane (Author)) or Twitter (@robertJcrane), or part of my Facebook fan page (Team RJC), it's easy to miss my book announcements because ... well, because social media is an imprecise thing.

Find listings for all my books plus some more behind-the-scenes info on my website: http://www.robertjcrane.com!

Cheers,
Robert J. Crane

Other Works by Robert J. Crane

The Girl in the Box
(and Out of the Box)
Contemporary Urban Fantasy

World of Sanctuary
Epic Fantasy

(in best reading order)

1. Defender (Volume 1)
2. Avenger (Volume 2)
3. Champion (Volume 3)
4. Crusader (Volume 4)
5. Sanctuary Tales (Volume 4.25)
6. Thy Father's Shadow (Volume 4.5)
7. Master (Volume 5)
8. Fated in Darkness (Volume 5.5)
9. Warlord (Volume 6)
10. Heretic (Volume 7)
11. Legend (Volume 8)
12. Ghosts of Sanctuary (Volume 9)
13. Call of the Hero (Volume 10)
14. The Scourge of Despair (Volume 11)
15. Rage of the Ancients* Coming in 2023!

Ashes of Luukessia
A Sanctuary Trilogy
(with Michael Winstone)
(Trilogy Complete)

1. A Haven in Ash (Ashes of Luukessia #1)
2. A Respite From Storms (Ashes of Luukessia #2)
3. A Home in the Hills (Ashes of Luukessia #3)

Liars and Vampires
YA Urban Fantasy
(with Lauren Harper)

1. No One Will Believe You
2. Someone Should Save Her
3. You Can't Go Home Again
4. Lies in the Dark
5. Her Lying Days Are Done
6. Heir of the Dog
7. Hit You Where You Live
8. Her Endless Night
9. Burned Me* - Coming in 2023!
10. Something In That Vein*

Southern Watch
Dark Contemporary Fantasy/Horror

1. Called
2. Depths
3. Corrupted
4. Unearthed
5. Legion
6. Starling
7. Forsaken
8. Hallowed* - Coming in 2023!

The Mira Brand Adventures
YA Modern Fantasy
(Series Complete)

1. The World Beneath
2. The Tide of Ages
3. The City of Lies
4. The King of the Skies
5. The Best of Us

6. We Aimless Few
7. The Gang of Legend
8. The Antecessor Conundrum

*Forthcoming, title subject to change

ACKNOWLEDGMENTS

Thanks to Lewis Moore for editing this book. Proofing was by Lillie of Lillie's Literary Service (https://lilliesls.word-press.com).

Cover by Karri Klawiter (artbykarri.com).

Co-authoring by Kate Hasbrouck.

Sanity NOT by Robert J. Crane's family. But I love them anyway.

Printed in Great Britain
by Amazon

84175456R00153